THE MOSES CHRONICLES: PRELUDE

RR WEKESA

RATIONAL FREE PRESS
BOISE · SILICON VALLEY · TORONTO

Published in the United States and Canada by:
Rational Free Press
1350 S Five Mile Rd #190771
Boise, ID 83709

ISBN: 978-1-7382891-5-8
Second Edition – 2026
Printed in the United States of America

For more information, contact:
Regina Roundtree
Regina@MosesChronicles.com
www.MosesChronicles.com

Contents

Dedication

To my mother, Prudence—I never realized how much I needed you until
now.
I miss you deeply.

And
To the men in my life who have made me a better woman— Charles, Ray,
Kevin, Neil, Lonnie
and last but not least,
Wesley, Bill, and Griffin

Acknowledgment

To my Apostle, for always "keeping it real". You inspire me to excellence, and I am grateful. Love and honor you, sir. Always.

***

To every person who has shared a Sabbath class with me on ClubHouse:

Whether it was the Sabbath Town Halls studies on Friday nights or the smaller 10/40 Window classes early Saturday mornings.

You have inspired me and challenged me to examine what the Torah is saying to us today. As a result, I feel free to dream and imagine what it might have been like to walk with the Patriarchs, travel through the wilderness, or cross the Jordan.

I pray this book draws you into a deeper relationship with Elohim, not because of doctrine (this is fiction woven with Scripture), but because, as you read this book, you will desire to see and experience your Creator in new ways.

Thank you.

Early Praise for the Book

"*The Moses Chronicles: Prelude* invites you to follow the biblical first family through their struggles to maintain faith in an ever-changing world. As a Jewish person, I personally connected to that storyline." — *Tricia*

"In ministry school, I learned to close my eyes and immerse myself in the text. The retelling in *The Moses Chronicles: Prelude* doesn't stray from Scripture—it draws me closer into the space between Scripture and story in ways that feel surprisingly like my own humanity: jealousy, uncertainty, unforgiveness, anger, weeping, love, faith, and forgiveness—making the characters feel more relatable."— *Michelle Spencer*

"*The Moses Chronicles: Prelude* offers a refreshingly restrained and historically grounded entry into the world of Exodus—without rushing into the anticipated and expected themes of slavery and plagues. What sets this first volume apart is its commitment to a slow, deliberate buildup. The Hebrews are not yet oppressed; they live under a fading legacy of Joseph's influence, in a society where political tensions are simmering but not yet explosive. The author wisely focuses on what could have actually happened in the Pharaoh's palace, the intrigue, the Egyptian power dynamics, and the quiet shifts that will eventually make deliverance necessary. It's a rational and thought-provoking beginning that respects both the biblical text and the intelligence of the reader, setting a strong foundation for the deeper drama to come." — *Neil Mammen, Renowned Apologist*

Author's Note

This work is a tapestry woven from Scripture, history, and imagination. *The Moses Chronicles: Prelude* is rooted in the final chapters of Genesis, where Jacob blesses his sons and is laid to rest—and where twelve sons, two nephews, and the women who love them begin to forge lasting bonds in the shadow of his final words. Relationships are given breath and depth, and the dynamics between them begin to shape a path that will alter the course of history—all while the sands of Egypt quietly shift beneath their feet.

I have long been drawn to the quiet spaces in Scripture—the places between verses where hearts break, heal, and hope. This novel lives in that space. While I've taken creative liberties to flesh out relationships, timelines, and motivations, I've done so with deep reverence for the biblical narrative and Elohim who authored it. I've also done my best to follow Egypt's pharaonic timeline where possible.

You'll encounter moments not explicitly recorded in Scripture or historical record—conversations, conflicts, and subplots shaped by study, imagination, and prayerful reflection. These are offered not as doctrine, but as fiction: an invitation to walk alongside familiar names and see them not as distant figures, but as living, breathing people navigating covenant, culture, and calling.

As I've often said: *I may take creative liberties with what is not said—but I never want to alter what is said.* That conviction shapes every page of this story.

This prelude sets the stage for what's to come—a sweeping retelling of the Exodus journey: from palace to wilderness to promised land; from promise to slavery to freedom. It begins not with Moses, but with the community that raised him, the world that shaped him, and the generations who carried hope long before he drew his first breath.

Thank you for stepping into these ancient days with me.

— RR Wekesa
Regina@MosesChronicles.com

Chapter One

THE FINAL MOMENTS OF ISRAEL

Last Sunrise

Dawn lay quiet over the camp, morning mist curling in the cold air. The scent of damp earth mingled with smoke from dying embers beneath the heavy linen of Israel's tent. Stillness pressed in—an unspoken expectancy. It was as though creation itself held its breath.

Isreal stirred on his bed, his once-mighty frame reduced to frailty, his breath shallow, yet his mind clear. His eyes, dim with age, blinked slowly against the faint light seeping through the fabric walls. Shapes were blurred now, more felt than seen. But he knew the sun was rising. He could feel its warmth edging closer.

He had lived long enough to see his children prosper in Egypt, long enough to witness the miraculous return of Joseph, his son whom he had once wept for, believing him dead. Yet even as he lay in the land of Pharaoh, his heart longed for the land of his fathers—for the resting place of Abraham and Isaac.

He knew today was the day.

He reached for his walking stick and made his way slowly, painfully to the tent opening. Smoke from early morning fires curled lazily into the sky, but the usual sounds of daily life—the laughter of children, the calls of servants, the clatter of clay pots—were absent. The camp was still.

Beyond them, standing in the distance like a reminder of a world both foreign and familiar, loomed the grandeur of the Egyptian palace. There, Joseph lived with his sons, Ephraim and Manasseh, dressed in the fine linen of nobility.

Israel's thoughts drifted like shifting sands.

Leah. His steady Leah, whom he had buried in the land of his fathers. He had not loved her at first, but she had borne him many sons and stood by him through years of hardship.

Rachel. His beloved Rachel. The ache of losing her on the road to Ephrath[1] still lingered in his bones. His heart clenched as he remembered the nights of longing, the whispered prayers, the silent grief.

Rachel had fought to be a mother[2] with everything she had, just as Leah had fought to keep him close.

He chuckled, the sound dry as dust. He remembered their arguments, their rivalry—even the absurd exchange of mandrakes, the odd price at which he had once been 'sold' for a night[3].

As his thoughts wandered further into the past, another face emerged. *Esau.* His brother, his twin, the one whom Elohim had not chosen. Had Esau truly hated him? Or had the years softened their wounds? He thought of that day, that embrace, that moment of unspoken forgiveness[4].

There was no anger left in his heart—only longing. And hope.

The sun crested the horizon, bathing the camp in amber light. Israel closed his eyes and let the warmth touch his face.

He was ready.

The sound of quiet footsteps pulled him from his thoughts.

Zilpah.

She moved like a shadow, appearing beside him with a basin of warm water in her hands. Her face, lined with age, bore a familiar look of quiet disapproval.

"Why are you up so early?" she asked, her voice carrying the sharpness of one who had cared for him for too long to be gentle.

Israel turned to her, "I must be ready," he murmured. "Gather my sons. Today, I go to my fathers."

---

1. Rachel dies – Gen 35:16-20

2. Rachel wants to be a mother – Gen 30:1-2

3. Sold for mandrakes – Gen 30:14-16

4. Esau hugs Jacob – Gen 33:4

Zilpah stiffened. The basin trembled in her hands, water sloshing over the edge. Her lips parted, as if to speak, but no words came. The shock in her dark eyes gave way to something more profound—uncertainty, fear.

For decades, she had served in this household, first as Leah's servant, and then as a mother to his sons, Gad and Asher[5] . But what would happen now? Who would care for her? She had borne him children, yet she remained a servant, a woman with no standing among the tribes of Israel.

She swallowed hard, pushing her fears aside. Stoically, she helped him back into the tent, her hands steady as she led him to the back room where the lamp burned low. She would do what she had always done — she would bathe and get him ready for the day.

A Father's Last Words

Silence enveloped the bed chamber. The dancing flames of the oil lamps threw shifting shadows on the tent walls. The air was filled with the aroma of myrrh and frankincense, blended with the subtle earthy musk of aged rush mats. Israel lay weak, his breath light, but his spirit was unwavering. This was a moment that could not be rushed, a proclamation that must be spoken before he was gathered to his fathers.

One by one, the sons of Israel entered, their heavy footsteps muted by the thick, layered rugs. His sons stood in solemn attention, summoned for one final blessing. Reuben, firstborn, broad and solemn, stood at the head of the bed, his jaw set, his shoulders heavy with the weight of uncertainty.

Simeon and Levi stood side by side, their expressions blank. They had always moved as one, their bond forged in the blood of Shechem. Judah stood tall, his presence grounded, as though he already bore the weight of leadership. The unspoken promise of kingship lingered in the room, though no words had yet been spoken.

The others followed—Issachar, Zebulun, Dan, Naphtali, Gad, and Asher—each carrying the weight of anticipation.

Then came Joseph.

Draped in fine linen, his presence was unmistakable. He was no longer the boy thrown into the pit, no longer the slave in shackles. He was

---

5. Zilpah's sons – Gen 30:9-13

Zaphenath-paneah, second only to Pharaoh, ruler of all Egypt. Yet here, standing before his dying father, he was once again a son.

And beside him stood his sons, Ephraim and Manasseh.

They were the youngest in the room—not yet in their twenties—but they carried themselves with the quiet strength of their father. Everyone already knew they had been blessed once already, in private, just days before. Joseph's charriot was unmistakable as it sat waiting next to Israel's tent. Israel had met with Joseph and his sons, laying hands upon his grandsons, declaring their inheritance among the sons of Israel[6].

Now, before all his sons, Israel would speak aloud the destiny of each one. His voice, though weakened by age, remained steady. Near his feet, Dinah knelt. She was his only daughter – the seventh child from Leah[7]. her fingers curled around his trembling hand. Silent tears slipped down her cheeks, though she made no sound.

"Gather close," he murmured, his gaze moving over them all. "Soon I will die and join my ancestors. Bury me with my father and grandfather in the cave in the field of Ephron the Hittite." Stepping nearer to the bedside, they all nodded in agreement.

Israel's gaze rested on Reuben first.

The Blessings of the Tribes[8]

Reuben – The Firstborn, But Not the Leader
"Reuben, you are my firstborn, my might, and the firstfruits of my strength, preeminent in dignity and power. But you are as unstable as water—you shall not have preeminence, for you have defiled your father's bed."

Reuben bowed his head, shame filling his eyes. Bilhah[9]. His birthright was lost.

Simeon and Levi – The Brothers of Wrath
"Simeon and Levi are brothers; weapons of violence are their swords. Let my soul not come into their council, for in their anger they slew men, and in

---

6. Blessing of Ephraim and Manasseh – Gen 48:1-22

7. Jacob's daughter – Gen 30:21

8. Blessing the sons – Gen 49:1-27

9. Reuben and Bilhah – Gen 35:22

their self-will they hamstrung oxen. Cursed be their anger, for it is fierce, and their wrath, for it is cruel. I will divide them in Jacob and scatter them in Israel."

The room tensed. The massacre at Shechem had not been forgotten[10].

Judah – The Line of Kingship

Then, Israel's gaze fell upon Judah.

"Judah, your brothers shall praise you. Your hand shall be on the neck of your enemies; your father's sons shall bow before you. Judah is a lion's cub. The scepter shall not depart from Judah, nor the ruler's staff from between his feet, until Shiloh comes."

A shift. A change in power.

Judah had been chosen.

Zebulun – The Merchant of the Sea

"Zebulun shall dwell at the shore of the sea; he shall be a haven for ships, and his border shall be at Sidon."

Zebulun's future would be tied to commerce and the sea.

Issachar – The Beast of Burden

"Issachar is a strong donkey, lying between the sheepfolds. He saw that the land was good and rested his shoulder to bear the burden, submitting to forced labor."

He would be strong but would serve others.

Dan – The Judge and the Serpent

"Dan shall judge his people as one of the tribes of Israel. Dan shall be a serpent by the road, a viper that bites the horse's heels so that its rider falls backward."

Dan would bring justice but also danger.

Gad – The Warrior

"Raiders shall raid Gad, but he shall raid at their heels."

Gad would be a fierce defender.

Asher – The Provider of Wealth

"Asher's food shall be rich, and he shall yield royal delicacies."

His tribe would be prosperous and provide for kings.

Naphtali – The Swift and Beautiful

"Naphtali is a doe let loose that bears beautiful fawns."

A free spirit, swift and graceful.

Joseph – The Double Blessing

---

10. Massacre at Shechem – Gen 34:1-31

Then, Israel turned to Joseph, and the tenderness in his eyes was unmistakable.

"Joseph is a fruitful bough, a fruitful bough by a spring, whose branches run over the wall. The archers bitterly attacked him, shot at him, and harassed him severely. But his bow remained strong, and the arms of his hands were made firm by the hands of the Mighty One of Jacob.

The blessings of your fathers shall surpass the blessings of the ancient mountains. The God of your father shall help you, and He shall bless you with blessings of the heavens above."

Joseph swallowed hard, gripping his father's frail hands. All the years of suffering, the betrayal, the pain—it had all led to this moment.

And then, Israel's gaze shifted to Ephraim and Manasseh.

Joseph's sons, no longer boys, but young men—young men who now stood as equals among their uncles.

Israel lifted a trembling hand, motioning for them to step forward.

"Ephraim and Manasseh shall be mine, just as Reuben and Simeon are mine."[11]

A shift. A change in inheritance.

Reuben flinched, but he did not protest. Simeon clenched his fist.

It was done.

Ephraim and Manasseh had been fully counted among the tribes of Israel. Joseph had been given a double portion.

No one spoke. No one argued.

Israel exhaled, his body sinking into the linens. Slowly, he drew his feet up into the bed, his hands falling still upon his chest.

A single breath.

And then, he was gone.

Dinah's shoulders shook as she clutched his lifeless hand. Joseph closed his eyes, his lips pressing into a tight line as he reached for his father's still fingers.

His father—the man who had wrestled with the Angel of Elohim and prevailed—had breathed his last breath.

The son who had been lost had returned. And now, he would bury his father with honor.

---

11. Ephraim and Manasseh are mine – Gen 48:5

Chapter Two

THE FRACTURED BROTHERHOOD

Alone with the Pain

The silence was broken by a single cry.

Joseph, the son once lost and then found, collapsed onto his father's still form, overcome by a raw, guttural wail that shook the tent walls. He clutched at Israel's linen robes, his face pressed into his father's chest—as if holding on could stop him from slipping away[1].

The others stood motionless. None could share this moment—not with Joseph, who had lost so many years with his father, who had lived as an orphan while the rest of them carried on.

One by one, they slipped out, their feet heavy against the woven rugs. Outside, the evening chill had settled in, but no one returned home. They lingered in silence, watching the tent as though waiting for grief to pass.

Joseph needed this time. It was only fair. And as the older brothers gave him space, a different weight settled on Joseph's sons—the burden of seeing their father undone by sorrow.

Near the doorway, Ephraim and Manasseh stood frozen, their youthful faces cast in shadow by the glowing lamplight. They had never seen their father like this. He was always the Vizier, always composed, always strong. Now, he was a grieving son.

They wavered, unsure of what to do. Should they remain? Should they speak? Comfort him? They had never shed a tear in public—not where

---

1. Joseph clings to Israel – Gen 50:1

anyone could see. To mourn as Hebrews mourned was foreign to them. And yet, tonight, they cried—not for themselves, but for the pain in their father's eyes.

Dinah stepped beside them, her demeanor gentle. She had never spent any time with Joseph, since they arrived in Egypt—that was almost seventeen years ago. And she had never seen his wife, but looking at these boys, she saw traces of her father. The tilt of a brow, the stubborn set of the jaw. *Strange*, she thought, *how Jacob's blood found its way into foreign frames.*

"Come," she whispered. "Give him time."

Manasseh clenched his jaw, his fingers curling into fists before he finally nodded. Ephraim exhaled slowly and turned to follow. Together, they walked toward the waiting chariot, their steps slow and reluctant.

It seemed like hours before Joseph finally emerged, his face drawn, his eyes red and shadowed. He straightened his shoulders, pressing the sorrow deep into his chest, and addressed them.

"He will be embalmed," he stated, his voice quiet but steady. "We will mourn for him here, but I will see to it that we take him to Machpelah, where he belongs."

The sons of Jacob nodded, though unease flickered in their eyes. The land of their fathers lay far from Egypt, beyond the wealth and safety of Pharaoh's lands. It was a journey that would not be simple.

Without another word, Joseph stepped into the chariot. Ephraim and Manasseh sat stiffly on either side of him, stealing cautious glances his way. The silence stretched between them, heavy and unspoken. They had no words for this kind of loss. They had spent their entire lives in Egypt, raised in palaces and educated among nobles. They had never known what it meant to lose the patriarch of a family—the father of an entire nation.

Finally, Ephraim broke the quiet.

"Father," he murmured, his voice uncertain. "Will Elohim meet him in paradise?"

Joseph inhaled sharply, then turned to his son, his posture softening.

"Yes, my son," he answered gently. "He is already there."

A Night of Reflection

As the chariot pulled up to the palace, the torches lining the entrance glimmered against the carved alabaster columns. The great stone columns towered above them, bathed in the warm glow of oil lamps. Even at this late hour, the air was filled with the distant sounds of servants moving about their tasks, the muffled murmurs of royal life continuing.

Inside the doorway, Asenath was waiting. She moved quickly as Joseph stepped down from the chariot, her face etched with quiet concern. She was not the most beautiful of Egyptian nobelwomen, but she was wise and kind. She had been chosen for Joseph[2] by Pharaoh—not for her beauty, but for her mind and her steady presence.

A woman whose strength had anchored him through years of political duty.

A devoted mother.

A faithful wife.

She embraced him before he could speak, and he sighed into her shoulder, feeling the exhaustion settle deep in his bones. Ephraim and Manasseh quietly left the chariot and headed to their room.

Inside, the warmth of a fire seeped against the stone floors. Asenath hurried to remove his heavy outer robe, her hands steady, but her eyes searching his. She did not ask, only waited, patient as always.

He sat on the edge of the bed, rubbing a hand across his forehead. "It is done," he murmured. "Father has gone to his rest."

She sat beside him, silent, waiting for him to continue.

Joseph let out a long breath. "Even as Vizier, I will need Pharaoh's permission to travel outside Egypt, to mourn, to bury him in Canaan. But... the weight of it all, Asenath—I feel like that young man again, lost in a prison cell, waiting on Elohim to guide my steps."

She reached for his hand, squeezing it gently as she pulled him under the covers. "Then you know what to do."

He nodded, whispering a quiet prayer into the stillness before allowing sleep to claim him.

Fire in the Village

Back in the village, the night was far from over.

The brothers remained gathered outside Israel's tent, a fire crackling at the center of their circle. They did not speak at first. Each of them was lost

---

2. Joseph's wife – Gen 41:45

in thought, sifting through their father's final words, feeling the weight of what had been spoken over them.

Israel had not simply blessed them. He had reshaped the future of their family.

Reuben and Simeon, the firstborn and second-born, had been set aside. Ephraim and Manasseh had taken their place.

The implications lingered, unspoken but felt.

Dinah sat just inside the tent, watching them from the shadows, her heart heavy with unspoken fears.

What would become of her now?

Israel's grace had been the only thing keeping her from complete exile. If they cast her out, would she plead for Joseph's mercy? He, at least, knew the wrath of their brothers. He understood how cold and unyielding they could be.

Benjamin was the first to break the silence. His voice was uncertain, hesitant. "Do you think Joseph will put us in slavery?"

Reuben turned sharply, flashing him a glare. Some of them scoffed, shaking their heads in disapproval. Others murmured among themselves.

"Joseph would never," one insisted.

"He is second to Pharaoh," another countered. "He is more Egyptian than Hebrew now. His children are foreigners and yet father blessed them. Why would he care about us?"

Reuben spat into the fire. "Father has left us no land to claim as our own. All we have is because of Joseph." It was the truth, but it stung. His name was barely a whisper in their father's final blessing.

Benjamin, his face tightening, snapped back, "Well, if you had not left him, things would be different[3]."

A sharp breath.

Simeon and Levi moved before the words had fully settled, their anger immediate, instinctive—a force unchecked by reason. Like two lions responding to a challenge, they lunged at Benjamin, driving him back onto the ground.

Gad, the warrior, reacted just as fast. He threw himself between them, catching Levi's wrist before the blow could land. Simeon's fist landed squarely on Benjamin's shoulder, but before he could strike again, Gad drove his forearm against Simeon's chest, forcing him back.

---

3. Reuben defends Joseph – Gen 37:21-30

"Enough!" Gad growled, his strength alone holding the three apart.

The others scrambled, pulling them apart, shoving them away from one another as the fire crackled violently between them. The air smelled of sweat and dust, their ragged breathing filling the space left by their father's absence.

Judah stepped forward, his voice calm but firm.

"Enough."

The fire snapped, casting sparks into the tense silence.

"This is not what our father would have wanted."

He looked around the circle, his gaze steady and unwavering.

"Joseph has never given us reason to fear him. Not then. Not now."

His words carried the weight of reason—the voice of a man who had learned from failure, who now chose peace over pride.

Reuben, still kneeling in the dust, lifted his head. His voice was hoarse. "And yet, our places have been given to his sons."

The words hung in the air, and Simeon, bruised and breathless, let out a bitter laugh. "Isn't that the way of it? First, our father loved Joseph above all of us. And now, he has given our inheritance to his sons."

Levi wiped a streak of blood from his lip, his voice laced with frustration. "We are born of Israel's house, and yet two Egyptian boys now stand before us."

"They haven't grown up with us and haven't shared our sufferings, our scars. And yet, they stand at the head of the line—as if blood no longer mattered," Dan murmured.

Judah inhaled sharply but did not speak. The tension simmered.

Zebulun, always the diplomat, shook his head. "The blessing is done. Nothing we say can change it."

Gad exhaled. "But what does it mean for us?"

Naphtali stepped forward. "It means Reuben and Simeon have lost their birthright. It means Ephraim and Manasseh will now stand as our elders, though they were raised outside our ways."

No one spoke for a long while. In the shadow of the tent, Dinah held her breath. She thought for sure they might turn on each other again.

Reuben sat back on his heels, shaking his head in disbelief. His voice was raw. "Joseph honors our father. He would not harm us, I know this, but still..." he trailed off, his hands pressing against his temples. "What do we say to him? How do we even begin?"

Issachar, who had remained quiet, exhaled through his nose, his mind working through the words carefully. "We must acknowledge the wrong we have done. If we do not, it will always remain between us."

Reuben swallowed. "Then tell him..." he struggled, rubbing a hand down his face, his fingers shaking slightly. "Tell him that Father left instructions before he died."

Issachar's voice was firmer. "Wait – tell him that we ask for his forgiveness." He put his hands to his heart, as if to summon the words. "Ask him not to hold against us the wrongs we committed against him. Not for our sake, but for the sake of our father."

A hush fell over them.

"Yes. That is the right message[4]," a voice whispered from the back.

The fire popped, sending a tiny spark into the air.

Simeon, glancing around, finally asked, "Who will take the message?"

From the entrance of the tent, Dinah stepped forward, her voice quiet but firm.

"I will go."

Burden of the Blessings

The breakfast chamber was filled with the comforting aromas of warm goat's milk, honeyed bread, and fresh figs. Ephraim and Manasseh sat at the long table, their movements subdued, their usual eagerness dampened by the weight of the past few days.

Asenath, seated across from them, watched them carefully as she placed a piece of fruit on her plate. The boys were not children anymore. Young adults now, standing on the cusp of manhood, but yesterday—yesterday had changed everything.

Ephraim broke the silence first, pushing his food around with his fingers. "I've never seen Father like that before." His voice was quiet, hesitant.

Manasseh nodded, exhaling. "Neither have I." He looked up, eyes dark with something unspoken. "He wept, Mother. I didn't know he could."

Asenath's heart clenched. They had grown up seeing their father as unshakable, always in control, always composed—the Vizier of Egypt, second only to Pharaoh.

---

4. Brothers message to Joseph – Gen 50:15-17

But yesterday, they had not seen the Vizier. They had seen a son mourning his father.

She reached for her cup, choosing her words carefully. "He loved Israel very much," she said. "Losing him after all these years... it was not the same as when he lost him the first time, but the grief is no less real."

Ephraim leaned forward, his fingers drumming on the wood table. "And then the blessing—before all of them." He glanced at his brother. "That was terrifying."

Manasseh frowned. "Did you see the way Uncle Reuben looked at us? And Uncle Simeon?"

Asenath did not answer right away. She could only imagine it.

The tension, the unspoken resentment. The shifting of power.

Ephraim and Manasseh had always known they were different. They had grown up in palaces, not tents. They had been taught Egyptian philosophy, politics, and warfare—yet their father always spoke of Elohim, of the people he came from.

But yesterday, everything had changed.

Yesterday, in front of all their uncles, their grandfather spoke the words that would forever alter their place in the family.

Ephraim and Manasseh shall be mine, just as Reuben and Simeon are mine.

They had replaced their father's elder brothers.

Manasseh's fingers tightened around his cup. "I don't know if I want that."

Asenath looked between them, feeling the weight of their uncertainty.

"You would give up that blessing?" she asked carefully.

Manasseh looked down, his jaw tense. "I don't know. I just—" He hesitated. "We don't even know them. Not really."

Ephraim exhaled, shaking his head. "They were always father's brothers. Now we're expected to lead them?" He scoffed, but the sentiment in his eyes betrayed more doubt than defiance.

Asenath reached across the table, resting a hand on Ephraim's. "You are not expected to lead them today," she said gently. "But one day, you will stand as elders among them. And you must decide what kind of men you will be."

Ephraim and Manasseh exchanged glances.

Manasseh exhaled slowly. "They don't trust us."

"No," Asenath admitted. "Not yet."

Just then, Joseph entered—his eyes rimmed with grief but dry now, as if sorrow had been carefully folded away.

The boys straightened instinctively as their father approached, his steps measured, his presence quiet but heavy. He met Asenath's gaze briefly before taking his seat at the head of the table. A servant immediately stepped forward to fill his cup.

Joseph took a sip, then glanced at his sons. "You're quiet this morning."

Ephraim and Manasseh looked at each other. Then Manasseh spoke. "We were talking about yesterday... about grandfather's blessing."

Joseph's gaze sharpened, but he remained still. "And?"

Manasseh hesitated, then shook his head. "We don't know what it means for us."

Ephraim met his father's eyes. "They were angry."

Joseph studied them for a long moment, setting his cup down carefully. "Yes," he admitted. "Some of them were."

A moment of silence.

"I don't think I want this," Manasseh admitted, his voice quiet but firm. "I don't know how to be one of them."

Joseph exhaled, leaning forward. "I understand."

He saw the weight pressing down on his sons, the uncertainty, the fear of stepping into a role they had not asked for.

Slowly, he reached for his cup again, turning it in his hands. "When I was your age," he said, "I did not know how to be a leader either."

Ephraim frowned. "What do you mean?"

Joseph met his gaze. "I had dreams," he said, his voice steady. "Dreams that I would one day rise above my brothers. I did not ask for those dreams. I did not want to be set apart. But Elohim had already chosen my path."

The room was quiet.

Joseph continued, his voice gentle. "When my brothers sold me into slavery, I thought I had lost my place in the family forever." He looked at them carefully. "But Elohim never lost sight of me. And He has not lost sight of you."

Ephraim and Manasseh exchanged glances.

Joseph reached for his son's wrist, gripping it gently. "Do not fear this blessing," he said. "It is an honor, not a burden."

Ephraim exhaled, his fingers tapping against the table. "I still don't know how to lead them."

Joseph smiled slightly. "Then learn," he said. "Watch them. Listen. Speak only when necessary. Leadership is not about standing above them—it is about knowing when to stand beside them."

Manasseh exhaled, looking down at his hands.

Asenath, watching them all carefully, finally spoke. "You are still young. No one expects you to know everything now."

Joseph nodded. "But one day, when the time comes, you will be ready."

Ephraim and Manasseh still looked unsure, but the weight on their shoulders seemed lighter.

A knock at the door interrupted the moment, and a servant stepped inside.

"My lord," the man bowed, addressing Joseph. "Pharaoh has been informed that you will seek an audience. You may come when you're ready."

Joseph nodded. "Thank you."

The servant withdrew.

Joseph turned back to his sons. "It's time for you both to go to your lessons," he said.

Ephraim opened his mouth as if to protest, then thought better of it. Manasseh sighed and stood slowly.

Asenath watched as the boys reluctantly rose from the table. Ephraim lingered a moment longer before nodding at Joseph.

"Thank you, father," he said, his voice quiet.

Joseph nodded in return.

They departed, leaving Joseph and Asenath alone.

She studied him for a moment before finally saying, "You did well."

He let out a long breath, rubbing his temples. "I pray it will be enough."

Asenath reached for his hand. "It will be."

For now, it was all they could do.

Joseph stood, his mind shifting from his sons to the duty ahead. He kissed Asenath on the forehead and walked toward the side door.

It was time to request permission.

The Back Hallway

The palace grounds stirred with the quiet hum of morning chores. Servants swept the courtyards, the rhythmic scrape of reeds against stone blending with the faint murmur of scribes exchanging morning reports. A pair of guards passed by, their sandals tapping against the marble as they changed shifts. Beyond them, the towering palace walls bore the unyielding gaze of gods and kings, their painted faces frozen in eternal watchfulness.

Joseph did not take the main hall.

He could not.

Not today.

There had never been a time he could not walk directly into Pharaoh's presence, until now.

His mourning robe—unadorned, its hem still stained with dust from the night before—was at odds with the brilliance of Pharaoh's court. His hair, uncombed, hung loosely over his shoulders, a stark departure from the polished state required of a royal official. The customs of Egypt forbade grief in the presence of the divine ruler. No man in mourning could stand before Pharaoh, lest sorrow mar the sacred order of Ma'at. Mourning was viewed as disorder—too human, too unpredictable for the palace of a living god. The priests upheld this separation strictly, guarding both Pharaoh's image and their power.

So Joseph slipped through the lesser halls, his path weaving through the shadowed corridors few men of his rank ever walked. Here, the world was quieter. The air cooler. The footfalls of the palace echoing in solitude. The shadows bent and stretched like silent watchers.

A passageway branched off to the right, one that was familiar. It led to the rear of the throne hall—an entrance reserved for high officials and royal kin who sought private counsel.

Joseph pressed his hand to the cool frame of the doorway before stepping inside.

Confrontation with Nefer-Ra

The chamber was dim, its walls adorned with muted murals of Pharaoh's conquests, their once-vibrant hues softened by age. A thick woven rug covered the floor, its fibers worn beneath the weight of those who had waited here before him—generals, scribes, noblemen.

Joseph sank onto a low bench, but the comfort of the cushions did nothing to ease the heaviness in his chest.

His father was gone.

The weight of mourning pressed upon him, but there was no time to be consumed by it. He had come to petition Pharaoh for permission to bury his father in the land of his ancestors[5].

But he would not see Pharaoh today.

Even in a private setting, Pharaoh could not look upon one in mourning—it was a sign of impurity. Instead, it would be the High Priest who would receive him, standing as an intermediary between Joseph and the throne.

Joseph exhaled, his jaw tightening. He would have no other choice but to deal with Nefer-Ra, the High Priest of Amun.

Few men in Egypt dared to show him open hostility, but among them, the priests and the magicians stood at the forefront. Ever since he had interpreted Pharaoh's dreams, the court magicians had regarded him with contempt. Joseph had proven them to be powerless[6]. He had done in moments what they, with all their spells and secret arts, had failed to do. His rise had been swift, and though Pharaoh favored him, the priests had never forgotten how he had humiliated them.

A rustling at the entrance made him lift his head.

Nefer-Ra entered, his robes flowing in heavy folds of white and gold, the sacred leopard-skin mantle of his office draped over one shoulder. His kohl-rimmed eyes, sharp and cold, locked onto Joseph's with the calculating gaze of a man who carried centuries of tradition in his blood.

For a moment, neither spoke.

Then, in a voice smooth as temple stones, Nefer-Ra broke the silence. His fingers brushed the edge of a gold amulet as he spoke, as though invoking unseen powers.

"Joseph, Vizier of Egypt," he intoned, his words measured, deliberate. "Why have you come before the gods in mourning?"

Joseph recognized the slight at once. He was not in the presence of the gods—he was in the presence of men. But Nefer-Ra, like all the High Priests before him, considered himself more than a mere servant of the divine.

Joseph did not rise to the challenge of the insult. This was not the time or place to start a fight.

---

5. Joseph seeks permission – Gen 50:4-5

6. Joseph's rise to power – Gen 41:8, 38-44

"I come on behalf of my father," he said, his voice calm and steady. "I seek Pharaoh's permission to take him home, to the land of Canaan, to bury him in the tomb of our ancestors."

Nefer-Ra studied him, his fingers still caressing the amulet. Then, ever so slightly, he smiled.

"Pharaoh has already spoken," he said smoothly. "The mourning for your father will last seventy days, as is custom. It would be improper to hasten the process. Would your father not be honored to receive the burial rites of Egypt?"

The words were careful, laced with hidden meaning. Joseph knew this game well. He was testing him.

"It is not our way," he replied evenly. "My father gave me his final command, and I intend to see it carried out."

Nefer-Ra watched him for a long moment, then inclined his head in acknowledgment.

"Very well," he said. "I will take your request to Pharaoh. You will have your answer soon."

Joseph bowed his head slightly but did not look away. He could see the disdain in the priest's eyes, the cold amusement lurking beneath his carefully measured visage. Joseph had no desire to be confrontational at this time.

Nefer-Ra turned and left the chamber, his robes trailing behind him like a group of snakes slithering away.

The Gathering of the Priests

Nefer-Ra stepped into the inner halls of the temple. The torchlights spew shadows across the sacred pillars. The flames pulsing to a rhythm only they knew. Several priests, their robes pristine and their postures solemn, gathered as he entered.

"The Hebrew seeks permission to bury his father," Nefer-Ra said smoothly, his voice carrying through the dim chamber. "Pharaoh will allow it."

The murmurs of the priests rose at once.

"Let him go," one said. "He will leave, and in time, he will fade from Pharaoh's favor."

Nefer-Ra's eyes cut to him, cold and sharp. "No," he snarled. "If he leaves, he must not return."

A hush fell over the room.

"He has ruled too long," another priest complained. "The people seek his judgment over ours. He is a Hebrew, and yet Pharaoh calls him his own. We should have ended his influence years ago."

"We shall correct that mistake," Nefer-Ra said.

There was a long silence before one of the younger priests stepped forward hesitantly. "Here, within Pharaoh's walls, he is untouchable. But if he journeys beyond—"

Nefer-Ra's lips curled into a slow, deliberate smile. "Yes. Outside of Egypt, on the road to his father's tomb, he will not have Pharaoh's hand to protect him. He will be vulnerable. The wilderness is treacherous. Accidents happen. An arrow, a stray blade, a fall from his chariot—"

"The desert does not return the dead," one of the priests declared softly.

Nefer-Ra titled his head. "Exactly."

A ripple of approval passed through the gathered priests. The plan was set.

They would allow him to leave. But he would never return.

Permission Secured

Hours later, still in the waiting chamber, Joseph sat in silence. His mind was weary, the grief still fresh.

A servant entered, bowing low. "My lord, the High Priest has confirmed your petition with Pharaoh. You may return your father to Canaan."

Joseph nodded and stood. He could still feel the weight of Nefer-Ra's gaze, the thinly veiled disdain behind his words. There was something about the exchange that unsettled him, though he could not yet place why. Outside Egypt, his title held little significance. He had faced hostile kings before—men who resented Pharaoh's reach and Joseph's influence. And now, he would travel far from Pharaoh's shadow.

Still, this was no time for suspicion.

He turned and left the chamber, stepping into the open air where his chariot awaited him. The journey to Machpelah had been secured. His father would be buried in Canaan.

And in the shadows of the temple, unseen hands moved into place, ready to strike.

The Taking of Israel's Body

The tent was heavy with grief. Ashes dusted the ground where Jacob's sons sat, their garments torn, their faces streaked with sorrow. Outside, the wailing of women carried on the desert wind, mourning for the great patriarch who had led them, who had once wrestled with anAngel of Elohim and prevailed[7].

Inside, Reuben sat rigid, his fingers clenched into the fabric of his torn robe. The others—Judah, Levi, Simeon, and the rest—spoke in murmurs, their voices laced with disbelief, with sorrow, and with something deeper. Something unspoken.

Near the entrance, Zilpah, the quiet servant who had once been Leah's handmaid, stood still, her hands folded in front of her. Beside her, Dinah remained silent, her eyes fixed on the body of her father.

Then, the priests came.

Their arrival was marked by a hush, a subtle shifting of weight as the brothers turned their heads. The Egyptians, clad in their pristine white linen, walked with measured steps. Their golden collars and bald heads, symbols of their office and purity, gleamed in the dim light of the mourning tent. To touch the dead was the sacred duty of the priestly caste, bound by ritual and rank. Their arrival marked more than honor—it marked control.

Reuben stood swiftly, his grief sharpening into anger. "What are they doing here?" His voice cut through the silence, rough as a blade. Simeon and Levi quickly rose to their feet.

One of the priests, an older man with deep-set eyes, bowed slightly before speaking. "We come on the orders of the Grand Vizier, your brother Joseph[8]."

The name was like a stone dropped into a still pond. A tension rippled through the tent. Reuben hated that he had no authority to stop them. He was the firstborn—but it was Joseph they obeyed.

"We have been sent to prepare your father's body according to the rites of Egypt," the priest continued. "Your brother has commanded that he be honored as a great one among us."

---

7. Jacob wrestles with angel – Gen 32:24-30

8. Joseph orders embalming – Gen 50:2

Reuben's jaw clenched. He glanced at his brothers, but it was Judah who spoke next. "This is not our way."

"It is the way of kings," the priest countered, his tone gentle, as if speaking to a grieving child. "Joseph has given his command."

The brothers were silent. What could they say? Joseph had the Pharaoh's ear. He had saved them from famine, given them a home in Egypt. How could they deny him this final tribute to their father?

And yet, it was not their custom.

Finally, Levi exhaled sharply. "Take him, then."

The priests moved forward with reverence, their hands precise as they lifted Jacob's body onto a linen-draped bier.

Dinah watched without a word. Her face revealed nothing, but her fingers curled slightly at her sides. Zilpah, too, remained still, though a quiet sadness touched her aged features.

As the Egyptians carried Jacob away, disappearing into the golden light beyond the tent's opening, the brothers sat back down. Their father was gone.

"This is not how it should be," Naphtali muttered.

"As if he were an Egyptian," Dan added, shaking his head.

"He will not remain in their land," Judah said firmly. "Joseph swore to us that he would bring our father back to Canaan."

The murmurs of agreement were subdued, laced with uncertainty.

Reuben looked down at the ashes on his hands. "Our father should have remained here with us until burial. But now he lies among foreigners."

"He is not with them," Levi murmured. "He is with our ancestors. With Abraham. With Isaac. His soul is not in Egypt."

The brothers fell into silence once more. Outside, the sound of Egyptian chants drifted through the air, a foreign rhythm to ears that had only ever known the prayers of their fathers.

Zilpah turned to Dinah and, for the first time since Israel died, spoke. "Israel has entered his rest; he knows not the turmoil of death—that is for the living to figure out."

Dinah said nothing. But she did not look away.

Chapter Three

A Sister's Plea

Facing the Unknown

The dawn air was cool against Dinah's skin as she washed her face, carefully braiding her hair with trembling hands. Almost seventy days had passed since their father's death, and though grief still clung to the family like a heavy fog, another fear had begun to settle among her brothers—the fear of Joseph.

Everyone became more easily agitated. Her brothers were always quarreling. It was like all the old wounds had been ripped open and healing was nowhere to be found.

Hope rose in her heart as she prepared to leave—not just to carry a message, but to reclaim her voice. To her brothers, she was carrying a message of peace for them. But the truth ran deeper. She needed to see Joseph.

Her father's death had taken the last shield between her and the full judgment of her brothers. As an unmarried woman had no standing, no inheritance. The brothers would not care for her.

Reuben would not, bound as he was by his disgrace.

Simeon and Levi? Never. They had spilled blood for her, but not for her sake—for their honor, their rage. Their vengeance had left her with the burden of shame, a stain upon her name from Shechem's destruction.

Gad or Asher might take in their mother, Zilpah, but Dinah? She had no one to claim her.

She chose her best clothes—simple, but well-kept. She smoothed the fabric with careful hands before stepping onto the road. She would not arrive as a beggar.

The road out of Goshen towards the city was well traveled. The cool wind rustled through the tall reeds along the riverbank, as she hurriedly made her way. She felt each step like a thump upon her chest.

Would he receive her?

Would he even recognize her?

At the Gates of the Vizier's Palace

The Vizier's palace was smaller than Pharaoh's, yet it towered over Dinah as she approached, its carved alabaster columns gleaming gold beneath the rising sun. Unlike the rough stone homes of the Hebrews, its pillars were carved with intricate depictions of grain, of canals, of the bounty Joseph had secured for Egypt.

Dinah slowed as she reached the great bronze gates, their height a silent testament to the power that lay within. Two guards stood at their post, dressed in fine linen, their spears gleaming in the morning light.

She had never set foot in his home, nor had she ever stood beneath the carved stone of the Vizier's palace. She had played with Ephraim and Manasseh when Joseph brought them to the camp, had laughed with them in the dust, but she had never met their mother—Asenath. The name was foreign on her tongue, and though curiosity pulled at her, she knew her place: not to ask.

One of the guards stepped forward, his voice impassive. "What business do you have here?"

She hesitated. To them, she was nothing more than another petitioner.

She lifted her chin, steadying her voice. "I bring a message for the Vizier."

The guards exchanged a glance.

"The Vizier is not receiving visitors today," the first one said.

Dinah's fingers tightened around the folds of her cloak. Did they know? Had Joseph told them not to let his family through the gates? Had he shut them out, even before she arrived?

She forced her breath to steady. "I am his sister."

The second guard narrowed his gaze. "The Vizier has no sisters among Pharaoh's house."

Her throat tightened, shame curling in her gut. Of course. To them, she was nothing.

She took a step forward, the boldness in her voice surprising even herself. "I am Dinah, daughter of Israel. I bring a message from my brothers."

The guards hesitated, murmuring to one another. Finally, one of them disappeared beyond the gates.

Dinah waited, shifting her weight, resisting the urge to turn and run.

A few moments later, the guard returned. "You may enter."

The gates opened, and Dinah stepped inside.

Awkward Introductions

The courtyard of the Vizier's palace was different from what she had imagined. She had expected grand columns and endless stone, a cold place filled with the weight of power. But here, there were trees. Date palms swaying gently in the morning breeze; their fruit ripening in the sun. The scent of myrrh and crushed herbs lingered in the air, mixing with the distant fragrance of fresh bread.

And then, a woman stepped forward.

Asenath.

Dinah's breath caught in her throat.

She was not at all what Dinah had expected.

She had imagined a woman of striking beauty, adorned in layers of gold, draped in silk, standing with the untouchable grace of an Egyptian noblewoman. But Asenath's presence was something else entirely. She was neither intimidating nor ostentatious. She was... gentle.

For a long moment, neither woman spoke.

Dinah's eyes flicked over Asenath's form, taking in every detail—the delicate linen of her dress, finely woven but unburdened by excessive ornamentation. The golden cuff on her wrist was understated compared to what Egyptian noblewomen usually wore. She was dressed as a woman of rank, yet without arrogance.

But more than her clothing, it was her bearing that unsettled Dinah. She did not hold herself as an untouchable queen, but neither was she meek. There was something about her—a quiet confidence, a presence that did not demand attention, but commanded it nonetheless. Not a woman who would sneer at her, as Dinah had feared. Not an enemy. This was a woman secure in her place.

Asenath, too, was studying her. Dinah—her never-before-seen sister-in-law.

The woman before her was neither an Egyptian noblewoman nor someone accustomed to courtly life. Her garments were travel-worn, the hem dusted from the road. Her sandals bore the wear of many miles. Asenath realized she had not arrived in a chariot or under escort, but had walked to this place of her own will.

And her eyes—they were not soft.

There was steel in them, as though this was not a woman who broke easily.

Joseph had mentioned her only once, long ago, in passing. A sister who had suffered. A name he had not spoken again. She wondered what Joseph had withheld and why. Was Dinah a wound left unhealed? Or a story too sacred to revisit?

Asenath felt a wave of uncertainty. This woman had walked from another world—one of tents, not courts. How did you welcome someone who had never been offered a place? *With kindness.* Immediately, her gaze softened.

"You have walked a long way," she said at last, her voice warm. "Come. Let me have the servants prepare a place for you to wash, and eat breakfast in the garden."

Dinah hesitated.

But something in Asenath's face put her at ease—not pity, but recognition.

She nodded, allowing herself to be led inside.

Joseph's Sanctuary

Asenath made her way toward Joseph's study, a quiet, secluded space hidden deep within their home, a sanctuary where he fasted, prayed, and studied in solitude. It was the only space that was indeed his, the only place where he allowed himself to be vulnerable with his God.

She knocked softly.

No answer.

Cautiously, she pushed the door open and stepped inside. The scent of aged papyrus, oil lamps, and faint traces of incense lingered in the air. The room was simple compared to the rest of the palace—wooden shelves filled with scrolls lined the walls, and a single bronze brazier smoldered in the corner.

Joseph had fallen asleep at his desk, his head resting on folded arms, his body slumped forward. His posture was not that of an Egyptian Vizier, but of a weary man carrying the weight of too much loss.

Asenath knelt beside him and gently touched his face.

His eyes fluttered open at her caress, blinking in confusion before focusing on her.

"Your sister is here," she whispered.

Joseph sat up suddenly, rubbing his eyes. "Dinah?" His voice was hoarse with sleep. "Why has she come? Is everything all right?"

"I do not know," Asenath admitted. "She only said she has a message from your brothers. I sent her to wash up and eat. She is waiting for you in the garden."

Joseph took a slow breath, steadying himself. He had not seen his sister in years. He barely knew the woman she had become. Why had she come now?

With a nod, he rose, brushing a hand over his face as if wiping away the last remnants of sleep. "I will go to her."

Difficult Conversations

Dinah was in awe of the luxurious home surrounding her.

The palace of Shechem had been fine, but this—this was something else entirely. The polished limestone walls, the intricate carvings of grain and rivers, the scent of blooming lotus drifting through the air—it was all overwhelming.

Servants moved swiftly, their eyes briefly lingering on her before looking away.

Pity.

Dinah was tired of that look.

She was tired of people treating her as if she were broken.

She followed the servant through an open archway leading to a lush courtyard. The garden was breathtaking—vines wrapped around columns, fruit trees cast soft shade, and a shallow pool reflected the morning light.

First they stopped at a stone bench by the far wall. standing next to it was a large clay cistern with clean water. On the bench was a clean towel and pitcher. Dinah washed the dust off her feet and face. when she was done they escorted her to the other side of the shallow pool.

A low table was set with an array of food—fresh bread drizzled with honey, plump figs, roasted almonds, and a warm cup of goat's milk. She hesitated. It had been a long time since she had eaten a meal prepared in this manner.

Before Shechem.

Before she had become an object of disgrace.

Her fingers trembled as she picked up a piece of bread, the honey melting against her tongue. She closed her eyes, savoring the warmth of the milk as it slid down her throat. For a brief moment, she let herself feel safe. Cherished.

Joseph saw her before she saw him—and stopped. He froze, taking her in as if unsure she was real. She was an exact replica of Leah. From the bottom of his soul a door opened and rejection flooded him. He remembered how Leah hated his mother and hated him.

Not wanting to frighten her, softly, almost like a prayer he whispered her name "Dinah."

When she opened her eyes, Joseph stood before her. She jumped up in shock, nearly knocking over the cup of milk. Then, quickly, she bowed to him, lowering herself in reverence.

Joseph reached out, gently taking hold of her arms. "Do not bow," he said gently. "Right now, I am your brother, not the Vizier."

Dinah swallowed, slowly lifting her gaze to meet his.

"You look so much like your mother," Joseph murmured, studying her face.

She blinked, startled. It had been so long since she heard anyone speak of Leah with familiarity.

They sat down, but for a long moment, neither spoke.

Joseph studied her as if seeing her for the first time—not as a child, not as a sister left behind, but as a woman who had endured pain and survived it. She was six years older than he, placing her close to sixty now, yet somehow, Elohim had preserved her youthfulness. There was a quiet strength in her eyes, a resilience that had not faded with time.

And Dinah studied him in return. It wasn't too long after Shechem that Joseph was pronounced dead to their father. This Joseph that stood before her now, she had only known him through the stories their brothers told—the lost son, the ruler of Egypt, the powerful one. Yet, sitting before her, he was something else. He was real. He was flesh and blood. He was her brother.

She remembered the few times he had come to visit their father. Each time, she had been hidden away, sent off before he arrived. Perhaps to protect her, or possibly because no one had thought to include her. It was possible that, even the night of Israel's passing, he had mistaken her for one of the servants.

A faint, sad smile touched her lips. "I know my mother did not care for you," she said softly. "She was often unkind. I do not carry her bitterness, Joseph."

Joseph tensed. He had known it, of course, but hearing it aloud brought back memories—memories of a mother who had never hidden her resentment toward him.

Dinah continued, her voice reminiscent. "Rachel cherished you like a king. She was never reserved with her love, especially toward me. Often, she would let me hold you while she looked on with great joy.

Joseph inhaled sharply, gripping the edge of his chair. The mention of his mother stirred something raw within him. He missed her.

His fingers curled into his palms, but he did not look at her. "You have a message for me," he said finally.

Dinah hesitated, then recounted what had happened that night at the fire—the argument, the fear, the plea for mercy.

Joseph stood suddenly, turning his back to her. His shoulders were tense, his breath uneven.

"Is that..." His voice broke. "Is that what they think of me?"

He squeezed his eyes shut. The betrayal he had long since forgiven still lingered in the air between them. Was it still not over?

Was this all that remained of his father? Suspicion? Fear? A legacy clouded by distrust?

He swallowed hard, wiping the tears from his eyes before turning back to her. His voice was steadier now. "Do you remember my dreams, Dinah? The sun, moon, and stars? The sheaves of wheat bowing before me?[1] "

Dinah nodded.

"Elohim knew then what He had destined for me," Joseph whispered. "My brothers only did what was orchestrated before time began."

---

1. Joseph's dreams – Gen 37:5-12

A long silence settled between them. Joseph motioned to a servant standing off in the distance. In hushed voices, a brief exchange of words, and the man hurried away.

Joseph turned back to Dinah and sat down.

"So, tell me, sister," his voice full of curiosity. "Why did you volunteer to bring this message to me?"

Dinah's heart pounded.

This was her chance.

She needed his blessing.

A New Beginning for Dinah

Dinah sat across from Joseph, her fingers tracing the rim of her cup absently. The warmth of the sun danced across her face, but her eyes held only sorrow. Slowly, her voice softened as she recounted the years after the family believed Joseph to be dead.

Her words grew heavier as she spoke of the continued shame of Shechem. Her breath hitched, and her speech slowed, laboring over the memory.

Joseph did not flinch. He remained still, listening, taking in every word. But deep within him, anger stirred—a righteous, silent fury. He was too young then to have spoken up, and even if he had wanted to, she was Leah's daughter. Rachel would not have allowed him to interfere when she had six brothers already.

After a long pause, Dinah exhaled. "I do not know where I belong now," she whispered. "Father is gone. And my brothers... they have never truly respected me after that."

Joseph sighed, folding his hands in front of him. "You belong here, Dinah. In my household, under my protection."

A tired smile touched her lips. "I am not a child for you to keep safe, little brother."

"You are my sister," Joseph countered firmly. "And family is not cast away. Not in my house."

Silence stretched between them, thick with years of unspoken wounds. Then, Dinah spoke again, softer this time.

"When we first came to Egypt, I was the one father sent to the market to buy goods and materials," she said. Her fingers tightened around the cup. "A few years ago, in the market square, I met a humble man." A small smile eased onto her face, as though just thinking of him brought comfort. "A tailor in Pharaoh's court. His wife passed a few winters ago, leaving him with two small children. He has been kind to me. I enjoy his company... and never once have I felt second-hand."

Joseph studied her carefully. "And you wish to marry him?"

Dinah hesitated, then nodded. "I do." A shadow crossed her face. "I tried to mention it to Reuben, but he would not hear of it. His defiled sister, marrying an Egyptian? He said it would bring disgrace upon our father's name. I never wanted that. And now that father is gone, I know they will cast me aside. I could not marry without a blessing from my family."

She braced herself, expecting to see disappointment in Joseph's eyes—the same judgment, the same shame.

Joseph exhaled, the weight of it leaving his shoulders slowly. Then, a gentle, unburdened smile broke through his grief.

"Then I will see it done," he said. "You will have a home, Dinah. A family. And his children will know they are loved." He paused, his smile widening. "Of course, Ephraim and Manasseh will want to see more of you."

Dinah let out a laugh, bright and full, ringing through the garden like the first break of dawn after a long night.

At the sound, Asenath emerged from the house, her eyes alight with curiosity. "What is this laughter I hear?"

Joseph grinned. "There will be a wedding," he declared. "We will have it here, in the garden. Something small, something ours."

Asenath gasped with delight, immediately sitting beside Dinah. "Oh, tell me everything," she urged, clasping Dinah's hands. The two women fell into easy conversation, giggling like girls as they whispered about the details of the celebration.

Joseph, seeing that they no longer needed him, quietly excused himself and made his way toward the waiting chariot at the entrance.

A Matter to Be Settled

As he approached, a guard bowed. "Has it been done?" Joseph asked.

"Yes, my lord," the guard replied. "Your brothers are waiting for you at your father's house."

Joseph nodded once, then stepped inside the carriage. His heart turned serious once more.

This could not be handled in the palace. Not where the walls had ears. This had to be settled—once and for all.

His brothers... after all these years, after all he had done for them, did they still believe he was waiting to take revenge? That he had only spared them so he could enslave them later?

No. That lie had to be crushed.

The carriage wheels rumbled against the stone road, carrying him towards his father's house.

The Gathering of the Brothers

Asher, Dan, and Naphtali had come first. Zilpah moved through the room, her hands steady as she poured tea, though her presence was as silent as ever.

One by one, the others arrived. Reuben was last.

"Has anyone seen Dinah?" Reuben demanded as soon as he entered. "Do we even know what has happened?" His gaze landed sharply on Zilpah. "What exactly did the messenger say to you?"

Gad rose, ready to challenge Reuben. "Speak to my mother with respect," he said coldly.

Asher, standing beside him, placed a firm hand on his shoulder, a silent warning to let it go.

Zilpah, unshaken, continued pouring. "The messenger from the palace said that Joseph requests all of you to be present this afternoon, as he will come to speak with you." She finished filling the last cup, then placed the pot down and left the room.

A whisper passed between Asher and Gad. "I have already spoken to my wife," Gad uttered quietly. "Mother will come to stay with us."

Asher gave a slow, silent nod.

No one spoke after that. They only waited.

The weight of uncertainty settled in the air, thick and unmoving. Then, the sound of chariot wheels approaching echoed beyond the tent walls.

The moment had come. The curtain at the entrance parted. Joseph stepped inside.

He had carried Egypt through famine, earned Pharaoh's trust, and sat beside kings. Yet here, among his own blood, he still had to prove his heart. He scanned the room, his eyes moving from face to face.

Not men. Not brothers.

No, what he saw were the faces of boys—boys who had once cast him into a pit. Boys who had betrayed him.

But also boys whom Elohim had used to save them all.

Joseph exhaled, steadying himself. He was humbled. Seventeen years. That was how long he had lived with them in peace—how long he had shown kindness, provided for their families, and asked for nothing in return. And still, they feared him.

Taking a seat, he folded his hands before him, inhaled deeply, and said, "Dinah has filled me in on all that happened the night of our father's passing... and the message she was asked to deliver to me."

The brothers stiffened.

The truth was about to be revealed.

Chapter Four

A Family Restored

The Dream's Meaning Revealed

The weight of silence thickened between them. Joseph could feel it pressing against his chest, the unspoken fears and wounds of years past swirling in the air. Then, suddenly, Reuben rose quickly from the floor, his voice desperate and urgent.

"We are your servants, my lord[1]."

A gasp rippled through the room.

Then, as if compelled by an unseen force, they all moved at once—his brothers fell to the ground, their heads bowed low, their hands pressed against the woven rugs. The very men who had once betrayed him—his own flesh and blood—now bowed low, declaring themselves his slaves.

Just as they had in the dream.

The one he had seen as a boy, the dream they had hated him for: the sun, the moon, and eleven stars bowing low. The sheaves of wheat bending to his own. He had told them of this moment as a boy—and they had hated him for it, calling him arrogant.

Dreamer.

Now here they were, bowing not to him, but to the will of Elohim.

Joseph's breath halted, his throat tightening as revelation crashed into him.

Elohim had done it. Not him. Not revenge. Not bitterness.

---

1. Joseph's brothers bow – Gen 50:18

Elohim had brought them here.

His vision blurred. His hands trembled. His brothers—his betrayers, his tormentors, his own flesh—were on the ground, declaring themselves his slaves.

"No," Joseph whispered, shaking his head. His voice broke. "No."

His body moved before he could think, in one motion he was on his feet. He took a step forward. His feet barely made a sound, but his breath was uneven, shuddering.

He reached for Reuben first, gripping his arms, pulling him up. "Get up. All of you—get up."

Still, they hesitated. Tears streaked their faces. Shame held them down.

Joseph's voice rose, but not in anger. "Do you not see? This was never my doing! This was Elohim!"

His hands clenched into fists before he released them. His shoulders shook, the emotions coursing through him like a flood breaking through a dam.

"Do you not understand? What you meant for harm—Elohim used for good! He sent me ahead of you to preserve life! Not just mine. Not just Pharaoh's. But yours.[2] "

Reuben's lips trembled, his hands shaking. "But we—"

Joseph cut him off, his voice thick with emotion.

"I was in the pit, yes. I was in chains. I was in prison. But I was never alone. Elohim was always with me! And now I see—he was with you too."

Levi let out a choked sob. Judah covered his face. One by one, they wept.

Joseph could not stop the tears spilling down his face. He did not try. The years of anger, guilt, and pain, the walls they had all built—it fell to the floor with their tears.

And then, they embraced.

The room filled with whispers of praise to Elohim, their voices raw and unguarded. Revenge, fear, regret—all of it lay forgotten on the floor.

A Bond Secured

Joseph wiped his face, laughing slightly as he shook his head. "Enough of this—we are family, not enemies."

---

2. Joseph comforts them – Gen 50:19-21

His voice softened, thoughtful. "And to ensure that remains, I have made a decision."

The brothers straightened, their eyes attentive.

"Ephraim and Manasseh are of age," Joseph announced. "It is time for them to marry."

Murmurs of agreement rippled through the room.

"I will not wed them to the daughters of Pharaoh's court," Joseph continued. "They are of Israel, and they must remain bound to Israel."

Silence fell as they awaited his next words. Then, he smiled.

"I will choose wives for them from the daughters of Benjamin."

It was more than a marriage—it was a seal—a way to bind his sons, born of Egypt, forever to the house of Israel.

A beat of stillness. Then—

Laughter.

Benjamin groaned dramatically, running a hand over his face. "Is that what this is? A plot to steal my children?"

"Why not?" Judah teased. "He's already taken your favor."

Naphtali smirked. "Benjamin, with his many daughters. Have you yet found the end of them?"

Reuben, for the first time in years, laughed out loud. "Truly, brother, one day the world will belong to your girls alone!"

Issachar chuckled. "Let us call for Zilpah and have wine brought. We must celebrate."

Outside, Zilpah stood still, her hands clasped before her. She had been listening, unseen, from the shadows near the door.

She had expected anger. Resentment. The brothers of Israel tearing into each other again, reopening old wounds.

But she had heard something else.

Laughter. Weeping. Forgiveness.

She had watched them tear each other down for decades and had held Dinah when they cast her out.

Tonight's laughter felt like rain after a drought.

Excitedly, she turned and hurried away, her heart lighter than it had been in years. Now, where could she find some wine?

A Celebration and a Plan

The table was laden with food, cups brimming with wine.

Simeon, for the first time, spoke meekly.

"And... what of Dinah?"

The table quieted.

Joseph could still see her standing in his garden, her voice trembling as she confessed her hope of marrying. A life stolen was being restored—not with pomp, but with quiet dignity. Joseph set his cup down, "She will remain with me."

He met each of their eyes, his voice steady. "She is our sister. She will be loved and provided for. You need not worry."

He did not mention the widowed tailor.

No one pressed him further.

Behind the curtain, Zilpah crouched in silence, joy leaping in her chest. And Dinah—no longer hidden in shame. Her name had been spoken without scorn. That alone was worth more than a bottle of wine.

As the night stretched on, Joseph shared with them his plans to take Israel's body to Canaan.

"We must be careful," he warned. "It will be dangerous. But I have already secured Pharaoh's permission. Many dignitaries will join us. A small army as well. The priests still watch me with wary eyes. And beyond Egypt's borders, not all foreign kings or traders remember me kindly."

At that, Judah and Zebulun stood.

"Then let us go ahead of you," Judah said firmly.

"We know the lands well," Zebulun added. "We will scout ahead and ensure it is safe."

Joseph nodded, relief in his chest.

Even now, after all that had passed, his brothers were still sons of Israel—bold, unwavering, ready to act.

And so, they drank and ate deep into the night. Outside, the sun had long since dipped below the horizon, casting the courtyard in deep indigo. The stars twinkled like diamonds in the sky—as if they too were rejoicing.

By the time Joseph stepped into his waiting chariot, his mind was hazy from the wine, but his heart was at ease.

The carriage rumbled through the empty streets, the stars above burning bright and endless.

When he reached his home, the lamps were low, and the corridors were silent.

A servant waited at the door. "My lord," he whispered, bowing low, "Lady Dinah is settled in the guest wing."

Joseph nodded, murmuring a quiet "thank you" before ascending the steps. His room was dark, but he did not need to see. His hands knew the space well.

Asenath was already asleep, her form curled beneath the linen covers.

Joseph eased into the bed, wrapping his arms around her. He pulled her close—warm, familiar, home.

His lips brushed against her hair as he whispered to Elohim, prayers slipping through his lips like a melody. Sleep claimed him before he could finish.

Not in years had his heart felt so light.

Anticipation

The palace was quiet in the early light of dawn. The air was still, save for the faint rustling of palm leaves outside the window.

Asenath stirred, her gaze drifting to Joseph, who lay beside her. He had come in late. She had not waited up, but now, watching him sleep, she could see something she had not seen in weeks—peace.

Even in slumber, his expression was light, almost content. The weight of mourning, the heaviness of responsibility, seemed, for the first time, to have loosened its grip on him.

But she could no longer hold her curiosity. *What happened last night?*

She had so much to tell him about her conversation with Dinah, but first—she wanted to hear everything.

She nudged him. "Wake up."

Joseph inhaled deeply, blinking against the morning light.

Then, a slow smile spread across his face. Not the cautious, measured smile of a ruler, but the unguarded joy of a man who had seen his family restored.

Asenath watched as he stretched, then suddenly jumped out of bed, laughing.

"It is done," he said, his voice alive with energy. He turned back toward her, eyes shining. "The seventy days of mourning have passed. And my brothers—Asenath, Elohim has done something I never thought possible!"

She sat up, tucking her legs beneath her as he spoke, and he poured out everything—the message Dinah had delivered, his meeting with his brothers, the weight that had been lifted from all of them.

Asenath listened intently, moving with his emotions—her brows furrowing as he spoke of their fears, her lips parting when he told her about Reuben throwing himself to the ground in submission. Her hands clutched the bed linens as he described their tears, their confessions, and their release from old burdens.

When he spoke of their laughter—the teasing, the wine, the plans for the journey ahead—she smiled, relieved that at long last, the shadows of his past seemed to have lifted.

But then, he said it—the marriage arrangements.

And she gasped.

Joseph turned toward her, startled. It was rare for Asenath to be genuinely caught off guard, and even rarer for her to let it show. But this... this was no small matter.

She swallowed, steadying herself. "You have decided on their marriages?"

His joy momentarily dampened by her sudden shift in posture. "Yes," he answered hesitantly.

"You arranged it already?" Her voice was calm, but Joseph could hear the tension beneath it.

Joseph tilted his head slightly. Something was wrong.

"I would have spoken with you," he said carefully, searching her face, "but it had to be done."

She exhaled, slowly standing from the bed.

"Asenath..." He reached for her hand, but she had already turned and was walking toward the open window.

She stared out at the horizon, gathering her thoughts.

When she finally spoke, her voice wasn't angry—only wounded.

She remembered the early days of their marriage—how he had sought her counsel on everything, even the curve of their garden paths. How he had once said, *Nothing in this house will be decided without you.*

Now, his silence felt like absence.

"This is not a minor thing, Joseph," she said quietly. "This is our sons' future. Our future. And you left me out of the decision."

Joseph's stomach tightened. He had never meant to hurt her. Never before had he made a decision about their family without her.

He stepped toward her, quiet, measured. "Asenath, I am sorry."

She turned from him, her arms crossing—not in defiance, but in thought. "Why so quickly? Why without me?"

He took a breath.

"Because it needed to be this way."

Silence stretched between them, only the morning wind slipping through the open window.

Asenath met his eyes, searching them. "I need to understand, Joseph."

He reached for her hands this time, and this time, she let him take them. His grip was firm, warm. Grounded.

"They are my sons," he said softly. "And they are sons of Israel."

Asenath closed her eyes for a moment, breathing in the words, trying to accept them.

She knew this about Joseph. She had always known.

Yet, something tugged at her.

"You truly believe they would not be accepted if they married Egyptian women?" she asked.

Joseph did not hesitate. "I know they wouldn't be accepted if they did."

She studied him, brows furrowing. "Pharaoh has favored you. The nobles respect you. Do you really believe that will change if our sons marry into the court?"

Joseph's jaw tightened.

"Yes," he said finally. "And even if it did not, I would not change my mind."

His voice was firm, but not harsh.

"I am not thinking of Egypt's favor, Asenath. I am thinking only of Elohim's favor. This path isn't only about marriage, Asenath. It's about covenant. The dreams I had as a boy —they're still unfolding.

A sharp pang struck her chest. *Elohim.*

The God of her husband.

The God she had come to respect—perhaps even love, though she still wrestled with understanding Him.

Still, a part of her feared what this meant.

"Then it is already decided," she said, more to herself than to him.

Joseph's hands squeezed hers gently. "It is."

She exhaled through her nose, shaking her head slightly. "You should have told me sooner."

"I know," he admitted. "And I regret that. But Asenath—this was never a choice I could have made differently."

She studied him once more, then let out a soft, almost amused breath.

"Benjamin's daughters?"

Joseph smiled, the tension in his chest loosening. "He does have quite a few, doesn't he?"

Asenath chuckled, shaking her head. "Your brothers will never let him live this down."

Joseph laughed, relief finally breaking through. "They already started with the teasing."

She sighed, but this time without frustration.

It was not the decision she would have made, but it was Joseph's—and if there was one thing she knew about her husband, it was that he did not make choices lightly.

Finally, she let her shoulders relax.

"Then we will begin preparations," she said. "I will speak with Ephraim and Manasseh myself."

Joseph kissed her forehead, deep gratitude flooding him.

"Thank you."

She arched an eyebrow. "I am still not happy you didn't tell me first."

Joseph chuckled. "I will not make that mistake again."

Asenath smirked. "No, you won't."

And just like that, the matter was settled.

Joseph had sought Elohim's guidance and would not compromise to align with Egyptian culture. And Asenath was strong enough to walk beside him regardless of the backlash.

Together, they would secure their family's future— not in Egypt's name, but in the name of Elohim.

Chapter Five

THE VIZIER'S RETURN

Back at Work

Joseph sat behind the grand stone desk, his fingers pressing against his temples as the day's reports piled before him. The past seventy days had been devoted to mourning his father, and though the rituals had honored Israel's legacy, Egypt had not paused. The robes felt heavier today. He was not just Egypt's steward—he was a son walking forward without a father.

Outside his chambers, officials moved in and out, each waiting for their turn to speak with him. Petitions, trade disputes, and land allocations—the wheels of the kingdom had kept turning in his absence, but they had done so with the quiet expectation that order would be restored upon his return.

The first matter before him was a dispute between merchants over grain shipments that had been delayed by the extended mourning period. One accused the other of hoarding and demanded restitution.

Joseph listened carefully; his gaze sharp but impartial. "Neither of you has suffered losses that cannot be explained. The granaries remained open, and rations were distributed fairly. No man will take more than what was given. The shipment will be divided as originally intended."

The two men bowed in agreement, knowing that Joseph's judgments were swift, fair, and final.

Another official stepped forward, bringing news from the Nile Delta. There had been unusual flooding, which had affected certain farming regions, and villages were requesting extra supplies.

Joseph nodded, already calculating the redistribution. "We will send reserves from the lower granaries, ensuring that those affected receive their due without compromising our long-term stores."

It continued this way, one matter after another, each requiring his attention. Although Pharaoh had the final say over all of Egypt, it was Joseph who ensured the kingdom functioned effectively.

And now, he had more than just Egypt's affairs to consider—he had a caravan to lead back to Canaan.

Strategizing for the Journey

After the last official left, Joseph turned to the head of security, a grizzled man named Amennakht, who had served in the palace since before Joseph's rise.

"We must travel lightly," Joseph said. "We cannot afford to draw unnecessary attention, but we also cannot remain unprotected."

Amennakht stroked his chin. "If you want discretion, I suggest a unit of six men, trained in stealth. Soldiers are useful, but too many will draw eyes."

Joseph nodded. "Agreed. We need men who know the terrain, not just how to fight."

"I have the right men in mind." Amennakht bowed. "They will be ready when you depart."

Joseph didn't voice his suspicions aloud, but he knew eyes watched him—from within Egypt and beyond its borders.

Joseph exhaled, grateful for the man's efficiency. The journey would be long and dangerous, but at least now he had trusted warriors to ensure his father's remains arrived safely in Canaan.

Dinner with Pharaoh

That night, Joseph and Asenath entered Pharaoh's palace for a private dinner.

The halls, lit by golden oil lamps, glowed against the polished limestone walls. Servants rushed about, bringing trays of fruit, roasted meats, and fresh bread.

Pharaoh sat upon his cushioned seat, watching as Joseph approached. The ruler's face was alight with warmth.

"Ah, Zaphenath-paneah," Pharaoh greeted him, using Joseph's Egyptian name. "I have waited these long days for your return to my table."

Joseph smiled and bowed. "The honor is mine, my lord."

Pharaoh's eyes twinkled as he gestured for them to sit. "Come, eat. Let us speak not as King and Vizier, but as men."

Joseph took his seat beside Asenath, and as the meal began, Pharaoh leaned in slightly.

"Tell me, my friend—how fares your family? I know you have mourned greatly, and I honor your devotion."

Joseph met his gaze, the honesty of Pharaoh's words touching him. "My heart is at peace, my lord. My father was given honor beyond what he could have imagined, and my brothers... they are adjusting to life without him."

Pharaoh smiled. "That is good. I have long admired how you deal with your people. Never have I seen a man rise so high and yet remain without greed or deceit."

He lifted his cup. "No one has ever come before me with complaints about you. No bribes. No favoritism. You treat both the rich and the poor with the same wisdom. This is why Egypt prospers," Pharaoh continued. "You have made this nation strong, and I will not forget it."

He leaned back slightly, swirling his wine. "Strong families make for strong nations," Pharaoh mused. "I trust your household is... united?"

Joseph dipped his head. "It is Elohim who gives grace. He has brought unity and healing to us."

Pharaoh chuckled. "Ah, your Hebrew God. You serve Him with such commitment; if only our priests had such humility."

Joseph chuckled lightly.

Then, Pharaoh leaned forward, his demeanor shifting slightly. "And your journey to Canaan? What do you require?"

Joseph straightened. "I have already secured a small unit to travel with us. My brothers, Judah and Zebulun, have gone ahead to prepare the way. I will ensure everything is done efficiently."

Pharaoh nodded approvingly. "Take what you need, my friend. Egypt will not deny you."

Pharaoh studied him a moment longer, his tone softening.

"One day, my son will sit on this throne. When that day comes... I hope you will still be at his side." Joseph bowed his head slightly, honored but silent. The request was more than ceremonial. It was a promise and a burden.

Judah and Zebulun Prepare the Way

While Joseph dined with Pharaoh, Judah and Zebulun moved swiftly, heading toward Canaan.

They had taken only a handful of men, knowing that speed and discretion were more valuable than a show of force. Their task was straightforward—to ensure safe passage for Israel's body and to establish a plan before the entire caravan arrived.

They traveled to Hebron, where their father had requested to be buried in the Cave of Machpelah. There, they met with local elders who still remembered Jacob's name.

One of them, an older man named Abdi'el, greeted them with respect. "Sons of Israel, what brings you?"

Judah spoke first. "Our father, Israel, has died in Egypt. We are returning with his body to be buried here, as he wished."

His head nodded in understanding. "He was a great man. His name is still honored among those who live here."

Zebulun stepped forward. "We must know the state of the land. Who among the people will stand with us, and who might stand against us?"

Abdi'el nodded grimly. "The land has changed since your father left. Some still honor the covenant made with Abraham. Others may have forgotten."

Zebulun's hand instinctively drifted toward the hilt of his blade, though he did not draw it. Judah's jaw clenched. "Then we will remind them."

They spent the night gathering intelligence, speaking with clan leaders and merchants who still owed allegiance to their father.

By the time dawn broke, Judah and Zebulun had secured their first group of allies.

While They are Away

Back in Egypt, Joseph and Asenath returned home after the dinner with Pharaoh.

Light from the wine, warmed by Pharaoh's favor—Joseph let the peace settle in, rare and welcome. Asenath watched as he unfastened his robe, then came to sit beside him on the bed.

"You are quiet," she murmured.

Joseph turned to her, a slow smile creeping onto his lips. "I am at peace."

She tilted her head. "Drunk?"

He chuckled. "A little."

She leaned into him, and he pulled her close, whispering quiet prayers of gratitude to Elohim.

Asenath closed her eyes, listening to the gentle rhythm of his breathing. And sleep overtook them in a cradle of safety.

Chapter Six

The Magicians' Plot

A Dark Opportunity

The room was dark, the only light coming from the flickering glow of a single oil lamp. The heavy scent of burning resins clung to the air, mingling with the musk of damp stone. It was a chamber hidden deep within the temple, a place where secrets festered, where jealousy and pride wrapped around the men gathered like leprosy consuming flesh.

The priests of Amun sat in a circle, their robes pooling around them like shadows. Nefer-Ra, the High Priest, stood at the center, his countenance carved from stone. Slowly, his fingers brushed the edge of a gold amulet hanging at his chest—an old habit when invoking the unseen. Around him, his council of magicians and scribes whispered among themselves, voices hissing like serpents coiling in the dark.

They had waited years for this moment. And now, the window was near—Joseph's caravan would leave soon.

The Hebrew who had humiliated them, who had stolen Pharaoh's favor, who had reshaped Egypt's future with nothing more than dreams and an unseen god would finally meet his end.

Nefer-Ra's lip curled as he surveyed his gathered brethren. "The Hebrew departs soon," he said, his voice smooth, quiet. "Out there, beyond Pharaoh's reach, he is nothing. A man, not a ruler. A foreigner, not a prince."

Murmurs of agreement rippled through the room.

"We will strike," Nefer-Ra continued, "and at last, Amun's justice will be carried out."

A priest near the edge of the gathering smirked. "And what of Pharaoh? Will he mourn his pet?"

Nefer-Ra's face darkened. "Pharaoh will mourn, but Pharaoh is a god. Gods do not dwell long on the death of men."

A younger priest raised his chin, eyes fierce with conviction. "Amun Himself foretold that foreign blood would poison the throne. What we do is not vengeance—it is obedience."

Soft laughter rose around them, but it died as quickly as it had come.

A sudden movement.

The doors burst open.

A figure stumbled inside, thrown forward onto the cold stone floor.

The priests surged to their feet, robes flaring, faces twisted in fury at the interruption.

"Who dares?" one of them snarled.

The man on the ground gasped, his hands splayed against the floor as he struggled to catch his breath—a spy—one of their informants embedded among the palace servants.

Nefer-Ra stepped forward, his shadow looming over the man like a cobra poised to strike. His voice was venomous. "You would interrupt us? Do you have any idea—"

"My lord!" the man rasped, cutting him off, his forehead pressed against the stone in submission. "Forgive me! But you must hear this."

Nefer-Ra's jaw tightened as he waved hand. "Speak."

The spy lifted his head, his face damp with sweat. His breath came fast, his words tumbling out in urgency.

"The caravan will not travel unguarded."

Murmurs rippled through the room.

Nefer-Ra narrowed his eyes. "Explain."

The spy swallowed hard. " Joseph's brothers, Judah and Zebulun, have gone ahead. They have already secured allies along the way."

The room stilled.

"The name of Israel is greatly respected outside of Egypt," the spy continued, his voice trembling. "And that is not all. Many dignitaries will be traveling with the caravan. High-ranking officials. Leaders from other lands."

A low hiss rose from one of the priests. "Even in death, the patriarch casts a shadow. Curse that name. They speak of him as if he were a god."

Nefer-Ra's jaw tightened, but he said nothing. The legacy of Israel still walked among them—and that was the true enemy.

A heavy silence followed.

The plan was unraveling.

A priest on Nefer-Ra's left shifted uncomfortably. "If we move against him now, it will not go unnoticed."

Another spat onto the floor. "This was our chance! Outside of Egypt, he is weak. But if he is surrounded by allies..." He trailed off, his frustration boiling beneath his words.

Nefer-Ra exhaled through his nose, his fingers curling at his sides. He had anticipated guards, of course. He had expected some level of precaution.

But this?

This was too great a risk.

No clean escape. No simple accident in the desert.

The plan had to change.

Slowly, Nefer-Ra turned to the gathered men, his eyes cold, calculating. "We will not move against him on the road."

A few priests protested, but he silenced them with a glare. "We are not fools. If we act now, we will be slaughtered like cattle."

Yet beneath his calm, Nefer-Ra felt the pressure tighten around his chest. He had staked everything on diminishing Joseph's influence. If the Hebrew lived long enough to sway the next Pharaoh... Amun's priests might find themselves bowing to a god they did not serve.

A pause. Then, Nefer-Ra smiled.

"But the journey is long. And long journeys provide opportunity."

The others leaned in.

"We will send two spies, embedded within the caravan itself. They will walk among them, eat with them, and speak with them. And if there is a moment-a single moment—where Joseph is alone, a dagger will find its way to his side."

A slow murmur of agreement filled the chamber.

One of the elder priests folded his arms. "And what of Pharaoh's men? They will hunt the assassin down immediately."

Nefer-Ra's smile did not falter. "Of course they will."

He turned to another priest, the one who handled temple finances. "Set aside a small fortune. When our assassin is struck down, his family will be compensated well."

"It is a death sentence for whoever takes this task."

The priest's voice faltered, his eyes drifting toward the darkened doorway—as if, for a heartbeat, he imagined his sons walking into death. "Must it be this way?"

Nefer-Ra stepped closer, fingers stroking the golden amulet at his chest. His tone turned to iron. "It is a sacrifice. One that will rid Egypt of this Hebrew blight."

Any remnants of doubt vanished. No one questioned again.

And so it was decided.

Two men. A dagger. A chance.

The magicians of Egypt had previously failed to stop Joseph.

They would not fail again.

Chapter Seven

FAREWELL AND A NEW BEGINNING

The Final Goodbye

The horizon had just begun to lighten, the sky shifting from black to deep indigo, hinting at the approach of dawn. The palace was still, save for the occasional whisper of sandals brushing across cool stone. Preparations for the burial journey would begin soon; departure was scheduled for the morning after. Today, the garden was being prepared for a simple ceremony: a wedding held on the day before they departed.

Dinah wrapped her shawl tighter around her shoulders as she walked through the eastern corridor. The air was cool, tinged with the scent of frankincense and cedarwood.

Zilpah walked beside her in silence.

They approached the chamber where Jacob—Israel—lay, his body carefully prepared for the journey to Canaan. Pharaoh's embalmers had honored him well. Linen wrapped him from his head to his feet. It had been seventy days and he did not stink. The bier was raised slightly, adorned with simple reeds and olive branches.

No guards stood at the door. Joseph had given the women this time alone.

Dinah stepped into the room first. Zilpah followed, her face pale but steady.

For a long moment, Dinah stood still. The silence in the room was profound—not the silence of death, but of reverence.

She approached the bier slowly, her fingers trembling as she reached out and laid a hand gently on the linen covering. She hesitated. Her throat tightened as old fears brushed against the edges of her resolve. Then, softly, "Abba...You are going home." A single memory flashed through her mind—his hands guiding hers as a child, helping her shape clay into a small lamp by the fire. He had smiled at her then, a hint of pride in his eyes.

Behind her, Zilpah stepped forward. Her face was drawn, aged with sorrow and strength. She placed a hand over Dinah's and spoke quietly.

"He grieved for you, even if he didn't know how to say it."

Dinah nodded, tears shining in her eyes. "I believe that now."

She bent her head closer, her voice soft and gentle. "I wanted you to know... I am not alone. A man has asked for my hand—not because of my name, but because of who I am. He has two little girls. I cannot give him more children, but I can teach the ones he has. I can give them Elohim."

Zilpah smiled faintly. "You will be their mother in all the ways that matter."

A long breath passed between them. Then Dinah stepped back.

"Go in peace, father," she whispered. "Your name will not be forgotten."

Zilpah stepped forward last. She did not cry. Instead, she stood tall and spoke firmly.

"I bore you sons. I walked beside you when no one else did. I will not walk with you to the cave—but I send my prayers before you. May you rest well with Abraham and Isaac."

Together, the two women turned and walked out into the pale morning light.

The Wedding in the Garden

As the sun climbed higher, the garden was prepared. Simple linen cloths fluttered in the breeze, and a woven canopy of reeds and date fronds marked the place where the ceremony would be held. Joseph and Asenath had kept it small—only close family and a few trusted friends from Pharaoh's household.

Dinah stood near the garden wall, the same shawl around her shoulders. This time, it was not for mourning, but for modesty and dignity. Her gown was simple but clean, the pale color echoing the hues of early spring.

Her soon-to-be husband, Horem, waited under the canopy with his two daughters. Nari, aged eight, stood straight and proud beside him, her small hands clasped in front of her. Kiya, just six, shifted from foot to foot with excitement, a crown of jasmine and rosemary resting askew on her curls.

Joseph stepped forward, acting not as Vizier but as brother, standing beside Dinah with a calm, joyful pride in his eyes.

He looked over at Horem and said quietly, "You've chosen well."

Horem bowed his head respectfully. "So has she."

The ceremony was simple, intimate. Joseph raised his voice only enough to be heard by those gathered.

"Today, we bless a union not born of ambition or youth, but of courage and kindness. Dinah, daughter of Israel, has endured much, and today she steps forward—not as one who was cast out, but as one who is cherished."

He turned to Horem. "You receive her not as property, but as partner, as wisdom, and as witness to the God who sees all."

Horem stepped forward and gently took Dinah's hand.

"I cannot give you more children," she said clearly, her eyes locking with his. "But I will raise your daughters in the fear of Elohim. I will love them as my own."

"And I will honor you as my equal," Horem replied. "And my daughters will know what it is to be loved by a mother who speaks truth."

Joseph turned to the girls. "Nari, Kiya—do you accept Dinah into your family?"

Nari nodded solemnly. "Yes." Kiya gave a toothy grin and ran to wrap her arms around Dinah's waist.

Laughter rose among the guests.

Asenath stepped forward with a small clay jar of fragrant oil. She anointed Dinah's forehead and whispered a prayer of blessing:

"May your household be one of peace. May your years ahead be gentler than those behind you."

The breeze stirred the reeds at the edge of the garden, carrying the faint trill of birdsong and the rustle of palm fronds. Somewhere nearby, a small harp played a quiet melody, its notes blending with the laughter of children.

Ephraim stepped forward and gently kissed Dinah's cheek, his eyes shining with warmth. Manasseh placed a hand on her shoulder and bowed respectfully. Neither spoke, but their gestures spoke volumes—acceptance, honor, family.

As warmth spread across the garden and laughter filled the air, Dinah looked down at Kiya's hand in hers, at Nari's wide, watchful eyes, and felt—for the first time in decades—entirely home.

The brothers had not come—duty and preparation called them elsewhere, readying the caravan for dawn. But they had sent word, their well-wishes folded into linen and sealed with their names. For Dinah, ac-knowledgement was all she needed.

And Zilpah—silent and steady in the shade—was enough. She had been there for the casting out. She had wept when Leah could not. And now, she stood witness to this special union—not as a servant, but as the woman who had mothered Dinah when no one else could.

Joseph raised a goblet. "To new beginnings!"

"To family," Asenath added.

Dinah glanced toward the garden's edge, catching Zilpah's smile. She nodded, emotion welling in her chest. She remembered those arms—how they had held her close through her childhood sorrows, through shame, and in silence. They had never let go.

And Zilpah, eyes bright, murmured a final blessing beneath her breath.

"To the daughter of Israel and Leah... may she rise in joy."

Chapter Eight

THE JOURNEY BEGINS

Lining Up

The scent of jasmine and fig leaves still lingered in the air from the day before. Dinah's wedding had been a quiet celebration—intimate, dignified, healing. Now, just hours later, the garden was empty, the linens packed away, and the house of Joseph stood once again in silence.

But outside, the valley stirred with life.

The caravan was forming, row by row—donkeys loaded with supplies, carts creaking under the weight of water jars and grain. Oxen stood tethered and calm. At the center, under a shaded canopy woven from reeds and royal linen, Israel's embalmed body lay in honor, perfumed and carefully wrapped for the journey.

The air was solemn, not mournful—the time for weeping had passed, seventy days had come and gone. Now, duty and reverence guided their steps.

Joseph stood near the front of the procession, dressed simply, though the leather of his belt still bore the crest of Pharaoh's court. He was not Vizier today. He was only a son.

At his side stood Ephraim and Manasseh, their cloaks fitted for travel, their eyes watchful. No longer boys of the court, but men of Israel—joining their uncles not in ceremony, but in solidarity.

There was no tension in the air. No unspoken guilt. No hidden rivalry. The sons of Israel stood together, twelve sons and two grandsons, bound not by blood alone, but by purpose.

Joseph let his gaze pass from Reuben to Benjamin, pausing on each face before settling on Ephraim and Manasseh—his sons, now counted among their uncles. There had been a time he thought this would never happen.

"Our father would be proud," Reuben said softly to Joseph, adjusting the strap of his pack. "This is how he would have wanted it."

Joseph nodded. "He always looked east." Joseph scanned the line, aware that not all dangers wore uniforms. The path ahead held more than dust and heat—some threats came cloaked in silence.

Simeon approached Manasseh, offering him a flask. "Keep this close. You'll dry out quicker than you think once we're past the Nile."

Levi motioned to Ephraim. "You ride with me near the middle. It's the safest place for the youngest."

Ephraim smiled. "Then I'll stay close."

Benjamin laughed. "You may be young in years, but in height, you've passed most of us."

Laughter rolled through the group, low and rich, grounding them all in something rare—joy, even on the edge of a dangerous journey.

Asenath had said her goodbyes the night before, wrapping her arms around each of her sons, whispering a separate prayer into each ear. She had kissed Joseph's brow and whispered, "Lead them well."

Now, Dinah stood silently near the palace gate, with Zilpah beside her and the two girls—Nari and Kiya—clutching her robe. She would not go with them. She had made her peace. Her life was here now. But she watched.

Joseph met her gaze from afar and offered a quiet nod.

Then, just as Zebulun reached for the reins of his beast, Dinah stepped forward, drawing something small from the fold of her shawl. It was a woven strip of blue thread, knotted with tiny beads and a single pressed sprig of hyssop.

"Place this at our mother's grave," she said softly, handing it to Zebulun. He looked at her, eyes glinting, then pulled her into a firm embrace. "I will place it with honor," he murmured.

Not far off, Zilpah watched the brother andd sister embrace, then turned to her sons. Gad and Asher were tightening the cords on their packs with practiced hands.

"Gad," she said, laying her palm on his chest, "you were born for the rush of battle. Let that fire protect your brothers."

Then, to Asher: "And you, my joy—bring light even when the road grows dark. Your laughter is a shield of its own."

She kissed each of them on the brow.

"Go. And return."

"Ready?" Amennakht, the head of Joseph's escort, asked.

Joseph looked out over the caravan. "Yes. Begin the march."

The Caravan

The first day's ride was steady and uneventful. They moved through familiar roads, past Egyptian fortresses and known watering points. The terrain was soft, the air warm but manageable.

At the center of the line, the bier moved slowly, honored by all who passed it. The soldiers flanked it without needing orders. The brothers rotated positions—some in front, others walking beside the body, each taking turns to honor their father in silence.

Amidst the servants, the two assassins traveled quietly. Neither wore Egyptian colors, nor did they stand out. Their names had been given to the escort captain days ago—scribes, supposedly, tasked with documenting the burial journey on behalf of Pharaoh. No one questioned them. They bore Pharaoh's seal, and that was enough.

They spoke little. One watched the brothers carefully, taking mental notes. The other remained near the pack animals, listening, always listening.

They asked no questions. They drew no attention.

No one knew that their true orders came not from Pharaoh, but from the priests. And those orders were simple: watch for weakness. Wait for the moment. Then strike.

Nightfall: A New Kind of Brotherhood

They made camp at the edge of the desert near an old well once favored by trading caravans. Fires popped as dry wood caught flame—the scent of roasting lentils mingled with the earthy tang of oiled leather and sand. Overhead, constellations shifted slowly across the sky—ancient and steady.

Joseph sat with his brothers around a low fire, its glow softening the lines on their faces. Ephraim and Manasseh sat close, listening, learning.

Reuben, watching them, leaned toward Simeon and murmured, "Do you see it? Ephraim... the shape of his jaw—just like our father. And Manasseh's eyes, when he listens."

Simeon gave a quiet grunt of agreement. "It's in them. Israel lives in them too."

Joseph turned slightly, catching only the tone, not the words. But he smiled nonetheless. Judah told a story about a donkey that once outran two camels and nearly tossed Naphtali into a well. Benjamin laughed so hard he spilled his wine. Even Simeon smiled.

There was no bitterness left. No old wounds reopened. Only a family restored.

Ephraim leaned toward Joseph, voice low. "It feels like we've always belonged."

"You have," Joseph replied. "You always have."

Watchers in the Shadows

They had pitched their small tent near the far edge of the camp, close enough to see the brothers gathered around their fires, but far enough to remain unnoticed. A dying fire crackled between them, casting jagged shadows across their cloaks.

The younger of the two, narrow-eyed and wiry, sat sharpening a dagger with deliberate strokes. His voice broke the silence first.

"They're stronger than I thought," he murmured. "There's no fracture in them now. No resentment. Not even fear."

The older one, broader in the shoulders, his skin weathered from years under Egypt's sun, nodded once, pulling his hood further down. "Time binds men together. Especially when their gods are involved."

The younger scoffed. "And yet they serve a god who hides in tents while we serve one who walks in temples of stone."

The older man glanced sideways, his voice low and bitter. "That 'hidden god' made a slave into a ruler. Never forget that."

Silence settled again, thick and knowing.

Finally, the younger asked, "You ever see him before? Joseph?"

"Once," the older man said. "Long ago. Before his family came to Egypt. Before the famine. He stood beside the High Priest of Amun and made him look like a fool in front of the entire court."

A long pause.

"I saw Senmut-Ra's face afterward. That day marked the beginning of the end for us."

The younger man leaned in slightly. "You think he knows who we are?"

"No," the elder replied. "And that mistake will end his life."

The younger sheathed his blade, eyes reflecting the low orange glow of the fire. "What happens if we fail?"

The older man's jaw tensed.

"Failure is not part of the command. The High Priest said it plainly—'No Hebrew shall rise again. Let Joseph be the last. Let no seed of Israel rule in Egypt.'"

The younger's brow furrowed. "This Pharaoh honors Joseph."

The older leaned in close. "Pharaohs will die. Gods will remain. The House of Amun forgets nothing."

They sat in silence again, the crackling of embers the only sound between them.

The younger finally spoke. "We will succeed. We've done this before. Crete. Amurru."

The older nodded. "And each time, we made it look like the wind took them."

Their eyes turned once more to the main fire, where Joseph laughed quietly with Ephraim, Manasseh, and his brothers. Their faces glowing in the light of the fire, unaware they had become prey.

The younger whispered, "And when will the wind rise again?"

The older smiled faintly.

"When the tent of mourning becomes a procession of pride. They will return to Egypt with carelessness."

Then they said no more.

Their fire burned low.

Their faces vanished into the night.

Chapter Nine

RETURN TO HEBRON

Threshing Floor of Atad

The land of Canaan lay spread out before them, a landscape of gold and dust beneath their feet. The caravan, long and winding, had moved steadily for days until they reached Atad, a threshing floor just beyond the Jordan. Here, they would pause for seven days of mourning, as was the custom of both Israel and Egypt[1].

The air was hushed with reverence. The sun hung low in a pale sky, and the grand procession came to a solemn stop.

Joseph dismounted first. He stepped toward the bier alone. The others held back, sensing he needed a moment.

He knelt, resting a hand lightly on the linen-wrapped form.

"We are on our way, Abba," he whispered, his voice thick with emotion. "Soon you will rest next to your fathers."

His eyes closed, breath slow. "Your sons have been healed and are united."

Then he stood, composed once more, and signaled for the others to follow.

One by one, the brothers dismounted and approached, the dust of the journey clinging to their cloaks.

Reuben was the first to speak, his voice rough with reverence. "Elohim has kept His promise. He brought us through bitterness and into blessing."

---

1. The threshing floor – Gen 50:10

Judah laid his hand over Joseph's shoulder. "And He brought us together—brothers once broken, now whole."

Benjamin stepped forward, whispering, "This is not just a burial... it is a homecoming."

And from each pair of lips, softly at first, then more strongly: "Blessed be the name of Elohim, who keeps covenant through generations."

Here, for the first time in the journey, the Hebrew and Egyptian customs merged into one powerful gesture of loss and legacy.

Clothed in torn garments, the sons of Israel stood shoulder to shoulder: no pride, no rank—only grief and unity.

They poured ashes on their heads. They fasted. They wept openly.

Judah's voice broke during prayer, and Simeon, once hardened and brash, held onto Naphtali as if drawing strength from him. Reuben knelt beside the bier for hours, whispering, perhaps apologies only Israel would ever hear.

Ephraim and Manasseh sat with their uncles, watching, learning. Manasseh took a turn pouring oil on the altar stones; Ephraim read aloud from the ancient prayers Joseph had taught them in secret. For them, this was a rite of passage—a binding not just to their uncles or to their father, but to Israel's legacy.

Officers of Pharaoh's court, scribes, and high-ranking officials stood in quiet awe around the periphery.

They had expected to see tribal customs that were rough and primitive. But what they witnessed was a mourning unlike anything they had ever seen in Egypt: deep, spiritual, and raw.

One nobleman muttered, "This is not the grief of shepherds. This is the grief of kings."

And so the place was named by the locals: Abel-Mizraim, "the mourning of Egypt[2]."

The Quiet Threat

On the seventh night, the spies watched from their camp, positioned a safe distance away from the firelight. Their robes were dusty, their expressions blank.

---

2. Naming the threshing floor – Gen 50:11

The younger one, crouched near the edge of a dune, murmured, "He prays like he believes it changes things."

The older one didn't answer at first. He watched Joseph as he knelt beside the bier, arms lifted, voice trembling in a prayer that seemed to shake the earth around them.

"It makes him dangerous," the elder said quietly. "Faith like that can defeat armies."

The younger spy frowned. "I've seen generals with less loyalty than these brothers have to him."

"He's not just a brother," the elder replied. "He's become a root. Cut the root, and the tree will fall."

They sat in silence for a while.

The younger reached into his pouch and pulled out a small copper ring, marked with a sigil of the temple of Amun.

"What if we're wrong? What if he is, in fact, just a shepherd whose heart is true?"

The older man's gaze never wavered from Joseph.

"Then House of On will reward us still and the gods will forgive us."

A Sacred Unity

That night, around the main fire, Joseph sat with his brothers, a cup of wine in his hand, though he hadn't touched it. His eyes were fixed on the flames.

"Tomorrow," he said softly, "we move toward Hebron."

Ephraim asked, "What will we find there?"

Joseph smiled faintly. "The cave. The promise. The end of a journey that began long before any of us were born."

Manasseh leaned closer. "Do you think grandfather knew we would come here?"

"I think he prayed for it," Joseph said. "And Elohim heard him."

There was no laughter that night. Only warmth. A shared fire among men who had been broken and made whole again.

The moon rose silently above the camp.

Somewhere beyond the reach of the firelight, two shadows blended into the night.

Still watching.

Still waiting.

Still dangerous.

Judah and Zebulun Scout Ahead

By the eighth morning at Atad, the desert winds had shifted. What was once a still and sacred space had begun to stir with movement again. Joseph stood at the edge of the camp, his cloak wrapped around his shoulders, eyes narrowed toward the horizon.

The caravan had traveled slower than expected. The weight of Israel's bier, the size of the entourage, the solemnity of the mission—all had slowed their pace.

Joseph turned to Judah and Zebulun, who were already preparing their packs.

"Ride swift," Joseph said quietly. "Go ahead of us. I want no surprises when we arrive in Hebron."

Judah's nod was resolute. "We'll see to it that everything is prepared."

Zebulun adjusted the leather straps across his shoulder, his vigilance palpable. "And if anyone forgets who our father was..."

"Remind them." Joseph's tone was not just firm, but a testament to his unwavering determination. "With words first. With steel if needed."

Judah and Zebulun rode swiftly, carrying only what they needed. The land grew rockier as they neared the hill country—scrub-brush terrain with scattered goat paths and stone terraces carved into the slope.

They arrived near Hebron in the fading light of day, the Cave of Machpelah nestled in the valley below.

At the outer gates of the region, clan leaders from the Hittite families and several local overseers greeted them. Most were polite, remembering the tales of Abraham, Isaac, and Israel—the foreigners who had once purchased land and walked with a God who fought their battles.

But not all were welcoming.

Tense Negotiations

In a stone-walled chamber near the city's entrance, Judah sat before a group of elders, laying out the terms. Zebulun stood beside him, silent but ever-watchful.

Judah's voice was calm but resonant. "It has been many years since the house of Israel walked this land. We return not as strangers, but as sons."

One of the elders arched a brow. "The land remembers little. Time moves forward."

Zebulun stepped forward then, his jaw tight. "Not all memories fade. We buried our mother here—Leah, wife of Jacob. Our father stood beside us as we laid her to rest. That cave belongs to our family.[3]"

Judah nodded. "Jacob, son of Isaac, son of Abraham, is returning to the land that was lawfully purchased. The Cave of Machpelah is ours—bought with silver. Witnessed. Recorded. This is not a plea. It is a covenant[4]."

One of the elders leaned forward, stroking his beard. "Time has passed. Land changes hands. Some may say the price must be renewed."

Zebulun stepped forward then, arms crossed over his chest. "And some may find themselves without hands to change anything if they dishonor the name of Israel."

The man paused, clearly measuring whether to laugh or not. But Judah's gaze did not waver.

"Do not mistake reverence for weakness," Judah said. "We are coming with Pharaoh's blessing and armed men. If you seek silver, you will receive what is fair. If you seek deceit, you will find war."

There was silence in the chamber.

Then an elder in the corner—a man whose hair was more white than gray—spoke at last.

"The sons of Israel have returned."

And with that, the tension broke. The others nodded in assent. They would not contest the burial. Not this time.

The Caravan Approaches

As dawn broke over the mountains, the caravan could be seen in the distance—a solemn river of movement across the hills. Chariots gleamed in the rising sun. Dust trailed behind the oxen carts. The scent of spices and embalming oils floated faintly in the air.

---

3. Leah's burial – Gen 49:31

4. Cave of Machpelah – Gen 23:17-21

Word traveled quickly. From vineyards to village courtyards, whispers stirred like wind through olive branches.

"So this is the Hebrew prince of Egypt..." murmured a shepherd near the outer wall.

Another, older man bowed his head. "The sons of the Hebrew God have returned. His presence walks with them."

Children were hushed. Elders stepped into the light. The air thickened—not just with curiosity, but with a sense of awe. It was not only a burial. It was the closing of a circle long left open.

Judah and Zebulun stood on the ridge, watching.

"They kept the pace," Zebulun said.

"Even with all the ceremony," Judah replied.

They did not wave. They did not call out.

They turned and walked back into the valley—not to announce the caravan's arrival, but to ensure that all was clear.

The gates of the city were opened. The people stepped aside.

And the sons of Israel entered Hebron in silence, bearing their father honor.

Shadows Among the Firelight

The night was cool, the air in Hebron dry and laced with the scent of olive wood fires. The camp was quiet—most of the men were resting in their tents or speaking softly near the edges of the stone terraces. The brothers had gathered earlier to plan the rites, and now, at last, the valley slept.

All except two figures seated near the back of the encampment, behind the shadows of a large cart.

The elder spy leaned forward, voice low. "In two days, they bury him. After that, the guard will thin out."

The younger glanced around, eyes steady but alert. "Then we strike on the way home?"

"We strike when he's distracted. When the mourning has passed, and their guards drop."

He ran a finger along the edge of his dagger, careful to keep it hidden under his cloak. "One cut, and it looks like a thief's hand."

The younger spy frowned slightly. "What about the sons? Ephraim? Manasseh?"

"They'll be silenced another way—if needed."

For now, only the night knew of their wicked intentions.

A Brother's Instinct

Nearby, Dan stirred from his place near the central fire. He hadn't been sleeping—not deeply. The rhythm of the camp, the silence of the hills—it had all felt wrong tonight.

He stood, stretching, pretending to walk toward the water skins, when he noticed the faintest glint of movement by the far cart.

He squinted.

Two men—neither familiar—were whispering, not like friends, but like predators. Dan had spent enough time fending off raiders and thieves during the wilderness years to know the posture of someone watching their prey.

He said nothing.

Instead, he turned, walked the long way around the camp, and approached Joseph's tent quietly.

"Joseph," he called gently from outside.

Joseph stepped out, robe drawn, his eyes alert. "Is there trouble?"

"Maybe," Dan said. "We may have an inside threat."

Joseph narrowed his eyes. "Go on."

"There are two men who do not belong to us. They speak little. They move like men used to hiding."

Joseph's brow furrowed. "You're sure?"

"No. But I've seen the signs before. Something in my gut says—we're being watched."

Joseph exhaled, then nodded. "Thank you, brother. We'll watch. But say nothing for now."

Dan gave a curt nod and disappeared back into the dark.

Joseph stood there, his hand tightening into a fist. He had known from the beginning. Nefer-Ra had never hidden it well—his polished words, his thin-lipped blessings, his eyes always watching like a serpent behind the veil.

Joseph didn't need confirmation. He knew the High Priest of Amun had wanted him dead from the first moment Pharaoh lifted a Hebrew higher than a magician.

But Joseph also knew it was Elohim who had elevated him.

Elohim had not brought him through the pit and the prison to abandon him in the wilderness.

He would be ready.

Above all, he would keep his sons safe. Because whatever hatred stirred in Nefer-Ra's heart, it would not touch Ephraim or Manasseh. Not while he was still breathing.

Joseph knew he needed wisdom. He entered his tent and stretched out on his face and began praying.

"Elohim…" he whispered into the earth.

A Day for Preparation

Early morning, Joseph stepped out of his tent, the flap falling shut behind him. He had fallen asleep in the same place he had laid down to pray after a quiet exchange with Dan.

The camp would rest that day after their long journey. Preparations had begun to clear a path to the cave. It had been sealed for more than two decades, and opening it would take time. Nearby, a narrow stream ran steadily, and the travelers made use of it—washing garments, bathing, preparing themselves for the procession that awaited them on the morrow.

Ephraim and Manasseh were set to the work of clearing rubble, alongside Naphtali, Issachar, and Benjamin. Donkeys were harnessed to carts, dragging stone after stone away from the mouth of the cave as a smooth path slowly took form. When the midday meal came, they ate where they labored, dust still clinging to their hands.

Night crept in without haste.

One by one, the brothers withdrew to their tents.

Yet Joseph's tent did not grow quiet. It remained a place of gathering well into the night. Reuben, Dan, and Zebulun stood just beyond it, speaking in low tones as they watched the edges of the camp. From time to time, a local tribal leader would join them. It was no small thing for the presence of Pharaoh to reach so far, and word had spread quickly. Men came with questions, with trade, with news—many seeking to speak of Jacob, whose name still carried weight in these lands. Others, dignitaries who had traveled with the caravan, requested private audience with Joseph himself.

At last, the final meeting ended.

Joseph sat alone in his tent, still and watchful, taking in all that had passed.

Beyond the camp, the hills of Hebron lay in solemn silence. Fires burned low, their embers dim beneath the deepening night. The sky pressed close, heavy and watchful.

The camp was quiet—but not at rest.

Joseph stepped outside once more, his gaze moving across the camp in a single, measured sweep. Then he turned and made his way to the smaller tent beside his own—the one where Ephraim and Manasseh lay.

He paused just outside, listening.

A Father's Instruction

"Do you think Father's worried?" Manasseh asked softly.

"He hasn't said anything," Ephraim replied. "But his eyes have changed."

Manasseh sat up in his bedroll. "Everyone's tense. The guards. Uncle Dan. Even Uncle Zebulun has been watching the shadows."

Ephraim was quiet for a moment. "There's more going on than we're being told."

Joseph stepped inside without a sound.

Both boys turned, startled but not afraid.

"Abba," Ephraim said. "We didn't hear you."

"I know," Joseph replied, his voice calm. "You were paying attention."

He sat between them, folding his legs beneath him, his eyes studying their faces—young, but no longer innocent.

"I heard what you said," he began. "You're right to be watchful."

Manasseh straightened. "Is something wrong?"

Joseph nodded once. "There are men in the camp who do not belong to us."

Their eyes widened, but he raised a hand.

"You're not in danger," he said. "But you must listen to me—both of you."

They leaned in, listening.

"We are strangers in this land," Joseph said softly. "Even here, in Hebron, even burying your grandfather. The name of Israel is respected by some… feared by others."

He looked at them intently.

"You are my sons. You are sons of Egypt and of Israel. That means you walk a path with no guide but Elohim. It means you must be careful. And when danger comes, you follow instructions—immediately."

Ephraim nodded slowly. "We understand."

Manasseh glanced at his brother, then back at his father. "Why didn't you tell us sooner?"

Joseph exhaled, the weight of years behind his eyes. "Because I wanted you to sleep soundly while you could. But that season is ending."

He stood, pausing at the flap.

"Tomorrow we bury your grandfather," he said. "And after that, we return to Egypt. But not all of us are here for peace."

He turned back, offering them one final glance.

"Be alert. Be obedient. Be sons of Elohim."

Then he slipped into the dark, leaving them with the silence of the stars—and the knowledge that something had changed.

Manasseh sat in silence, staring at the closed flap. Ephraim whispered, almost to himself, "Not all enemies wear armor."

Manasseh gave a slight nod, the light from the lamp catching the edge of his jaw. "Remember when Pharaoh assigned his guards to train us? We were what—ten? Eleven?"

"Too young," Ephraim said with a smirk. "But we held our ground."

"General Djet made us fight blindfolded," Manasseh added. "Said, 'A prince of Egypt must see with more than his eyes.'"

"And father said," Ephraim continued, lowering his voice in imitation, " 'A son of Israel must listen to Elohim before he lifts a blade.'"

Manasseh exhaled, his body relaxing into his bedroll, hands behind his head.

"We're not boys anymore."

"No," Ephraim said. "We're ready."

They turned over on their beds, eyes open to the dancing light from the lamp on the tent walls, the weight of their father's words still pressing on their chests—but no longer with fear.

With resolve.

Chapter Ten

The Burial and a Mother Remembered

The Cave of Machpelah

Morning came quietly and pale. The sun crested the hills of Hebron gently, as if in mourning also. The winds carried no dust, only stillness.

The sons of Israel rose early, washed in silence. Together, they prepared their father's body one final time. The linen was clean, the oils refreshed.

The procession to the cave was not loud or grand. It was deeply reverent.

Joseph walked at the front, Ephraim and Manasseh at his sides — no longer just sons, but representatives of the next generation. The bier was carried with solemn strength by Reuben, Simeon, Levi, Judah, Issachar, and Zebulun—each moving in rhythm, each carrying more than just their father's remains. They carried his memory. His legacy. His name.

As they neared the cave, Issachar found his gaze lifting—not toward the bier, but to the gravings above the cave's mouth.

Abraham. Isaac. Israel (freshly carved).

The names echoed in his mind like footsteps on sacred ground. These were not just ancestors—they were covenant-bearers. And now, they were being joined by their son.

Elohim keeps His promises, he thought, *even across generations.*

The Cave of Machpelah waited—unchanged, as it had been since Abraham first purchased it generations ago. Within it lay the bones of giants including his mother.

Now, Israel would join her again.

The Honoring of a Patriarch

Before the body entered, the procession halted at the mouth of the cave. Joseph and his brothers formed a half cirlce off to the side. Joseph in the middle and his sons on either side of him. One by one, those who had come with the brothers—Egyptian officials, high-born courtiers, captains of Pharaoh's guard, priests, and scribes—stepped forward.

They came not as conquerors, nor rulers, but as mourners.

Some laid down jewels, others rings of silver, or small carved scarabs bearing prayers of peace and protection. A handful poured libations of wine into the earth. Others laid woven offerings of papyrus and linen, items reserved for priests and nobles.

And nearly all of them turned to Joseph, bowing—not with Egyptian pomp, but with genuine reverence.

Joseph felt his breath catch. Egyptians—nobles, priests, warriors—bowing before the memory of a Hebrew shepherd, and unknowingly honoring the God of Abraham. *Elohim... how great You are*, he thought. *You've done what I never could.*

"Your father was a great man," one elder said. "And you are greater still for honoring him in this way."

"May the God of your fathers bless your line," another added.

The gifts began to pile up at Joseph's feet, but he made no move to gather them. He bowed his head in silent humility, tears welling up at the corners of his eyes.

The Sons of Promise

After the final blessing was spoken, Joseph stepped forward and laid his hand on the bier.

"Return, my father," he whispered, "to the land promised to you."

Then, with quiet care, they laid Israel in a carved hollow within the stone chamber, among the resting places of those who had come before him. Abraham and Sarah. Isaac and Rebekah. Leah, the wife who bore him half a nation.

His body was placed with reverence in the family tomb—not alone, but among the patriarchs and matriarchs of generations past. For a long moment, no one spoke.

Then Ephraim and Manasseh stepped closer, staring at the cave that held their Hebrew ancestors.

Manasseh whispered, "It's like walking through history."

Ephraim didn't respond at first. His eyes scanned the ancient markers, the time-worn carvings along the cave wall. The place felt alive—with memory, with promise, with presence.

Joseph approached and stood behind them.

"Here lie Abraham, Isaac, and now Israel," he said quietly. "These are your ancestors—not by blood alone, but by covenant."

Ephraim finally turned to his father. "Then this land... it belongs to us too?"

Joseph smiled faintly. "Not yet. But one day. When Elohim says the time is right."

Manasseh looked back at the path they had come from. "Will Pharaoh let us return?"

Joseph's eyes darkened slightly with thought. "He will—for now. But even Pharaohs forget."

He placed his hands on their shoulders.

"Never forget this place. And never forget who you are." As the light of morning deepened, the brothers began to turn away, one by one.

Israel had returned to the land of promise. And with him, the memory of everything that had come before.

The Matriarch Remembered

After the burial ceremony for Israel, as the last of the dignitaries departed, six sons of Leah remained behind. The others had gone to tend to the animals and prepare for the night's camp. But Leah's sons—Reuben, Simeon, Levi, Judah, Issachar, and Zebulun—lingered near the mouth of the cave.

They waited until the final ceremonial lamps had been extinguished and the area had cleared.

Then, silently, they stepped inside.

The cave was cool and still, the air thick with the scent of old stone, cedar resin, and ancient dust. Their sandals scuffed softly across the smooth, packed earth.

Inside, the chamber widened slightly, revealing rows of stone niches carved directly into the rock. Each niche bore a simple mark—a line, a name, a symbol—and shallow grooves where small oil lamps once sat.

A single lamp remained lit near the back.

They approached it in silence.

There, in a low, gently arched niche, rested a stone marker.

Leah.

She had been laid there years ago, before the long years of Egypt. Her place was quiet, honored, and undisturbed.

Reuben knelt slowly. He said nothing at first, only touched the edge of the stone.

"I remember your stories by firelight. The way you sang to me when I had a fever as a boy."

He paused.

"I was never the man I should have been. I'm sorry," he whispered.

Simeon stood nearby, arms folded, the lamplight dancing across his stern face.

"You were stronger than we could possibly understand," he muttered. "They said Rachel was beautiful. But you... you endured." His voice faltered. "I wish I had honored you more while you lived."

Levi placed a folded linen cloth near the base of her tomb. "Abba said my anger consumes me," he said softly. "But you always knew how to soothe me."

Judah knelt beside Reuben. "Your name wasn't sung like Rachel's. But it was your sons who carried father home." He placed a carved stone near the lamp. "I named my youngest daughter after you. Did you know that?"

Issachar and Zebulun each stepped forward with small tokens—dried figs wrapped in cloth, a carved shell from their old homeland, one smooth stone from the riverbed of Penuel.

Zebulun paused, then reached into his tunic and withdrew a woven strip of blue thread, knotted with tiny beads and a single pressed sprig of hyssop.

"From Dinah," he said softly.

"I was born from your prayer," Issachar whispered. "That you might earn father's love. But you gave it to us freely."

They stood together in silence, the air thick with childhood memories.

"She was never the favorite," Judah said quietly, "but she was the mother of half a nation."

Reuben exhaled and rose to his feet. "She deserves more than we gave her."

"We give it now," Levi replied.

One by one, they turned and left the chamber, their steps soft, their heads bowed—not in shame, but in reverence.

As they emerged from the cave, the stars had begun to pierce the twilight. Behind them, in the cool, sacred darkness, Leah's lamp continued to burn.

Outside, they marked the site with a circle of smooth, white stones—a sign of honor, memory, and promise. Stones were rolled into place and the entrance sealed, the sons of Leah headed back towards the camp.

Chapter Eleven

SHADOWS IN THE CAMP

Strategy Circle

Evening settled over Hebron with a hush, the last rays of light slipping over the burial ridge where the Cave of Machpelah now stood sealed behind its heavy stone. The air smelled of olive wood, smoke, and dry grass. The ceremony was over, but Joseph's mind remained restless.

He stepped away from the others just before dusk, his cloak drawn tightly against the cool wind. He met Dan in a cluster of trees a short distance from the camp, where three trusted men stood waiting—his hand-picked security detail.

"Report," Joseph said.

One of the guards, a Nubian-born scout named Seram, spoke first. "We've adjusted the rotation as you asked. No one outside the escort gets closer than twenty paces without being noticed. We change patterns every third hour. Also six men in total will remain closest to you throughout the journey back: quiet, loyal men who could move as quickly through shadows as through a royal court."

Another added, "The two foreigners—scribes, they claim. They sleep lightly and keep their gear close at hand at all times. No one has seen them slipping away yet, but they're careful. Too careful."

Dan crossed his arms. "They haven't made a move, but they're watching us as if they're waiting for something."

Joseph nodded slowly. "They know the time for mourning has passed. They may assume my guard will come down."

"But it will not," Dan said, firmly.

Joseph looked each of his guards in the eye. "If they move, I want it handled quietly. No chaos. No panic. This journey ends in peace, not blood."

He turned to Dan. "Position Ephraim and Manasseh near the rear guard tomorrow. Keep them away from the center where I ride."

"They won't like it," Dan said. "But they'll obey."

"I'd rather them angry than dead," Joseph replied.

Then, quietly as if speaking only to himself, "I want to return to Egypt with all my brothers. No empty saddles."

The Spies Wait

The night air hung cool over Hebron, the hills hushed beneath a sky pierced with stars. Near the edge of the camp, beyond the outer circle of torches, two figures sat in partial shadow, their fire reduced to a few glowing embers buried beneath sand and ash.

The older one crouched low, sharpening a small, curved blade with slow, methodical strokes. His eyes never left the firelight below, where Joseph sat among his brothers, shoulders bowed, gaze distant.

"He sits like a man who's finished something," the younger muttered, rolling a small date pit between his fingers. "Like a king who's won a war."

The younger let out a short breath, almost a laugh. "They all came—Egyptians, Hebrews, even old nobles from the court. I saw many of them leave an offering at his feet."

"Grief makes men foolish," the elder replied. "And fools are easiest to kill."

They both looked out toward the cave. The stones had been rolled into place. Israel was buried now. The mourning would soon give way to celebration, relief, and complacency.

"Do we move soon?" the younger asked. He picked up a stone and tossed it absently down the slope. The older man didn't respond at first. He finished one final stroke on the blade and tucked it away.

"No," the older said. "Not here. Not while they still remember the weight of his name. Let them sing his praises a few more days. Let them return to Egypt believing they've secured peace and success."

He pulled a folded scrap of parchment from his tunic; it was sealed with the temple's sigil at On. He unfolded it briefly in the firelight, letting the words glare back at him

Let no seed of Israel rule in Egypt again.

He tucked it away again. "We move when the trail grows long, and eyes grow tired."

The younger nodded once. "He'll never see it coming."

The elder smirked faintly. "That's the power of grief. It opens the door."

Below them, the fire crackled. The weight of the burial still hung over the people.

But the shadows were patient.

They would wait.

And when the time came, they would strike.

Rachel

The morning after Israel's burial, the sun rose calm and golden. The hush of the hills gave way to the quiet sounds of packing—leather straps tightened, animals fed, tents rolled up. The sacred stillness around the Cave of Machpelah was fading now, replaced by the movement of return.

Joseph sat cross-legged on the earth, surrounded by his brothers. A breakfast of lentils, bread, and dates was shared over a simple cloth. Nearby, Ephraim and Manasseh sat eating silently, their gazes still lingering on the cave behind them.

The conversation was soft, mostly logistical: how far to the next spring, what path to take, which guards would ride forward. But as the final crust of bread passed through his hands, Benjamin looked up, his voice low and unexpected.

"Where was she buried?" he asked, "... my mother."

The words cut through the morning.

The brothers stilled.

Benjamin, Joseph's younger brother and the last child of Rachel, kept his eyes to the ground.

Reuben looked to Levi. Simeon looked away.

Joseph glanced around, searching their faces. "I remember... crying. And Jacob's silence. But after the pit..." He shook his head slowly. "Besides the dreams, I can't remember much. I never knew what was real and what I imagined."

It was Levi who finally answered. He leaned forward, his voice steady, gentle.

"She died on the road," he said. "We were traveling south from Bethel. It was her time—she went into labor near Ephrath. The pain was long... violent. She was gone before nightfall[1]."

Joseph's jaw tightened. "And no one ever went back?"

"No," Levi said. " Israel buried her there. Set a stone to mark the place. But we didn't stay. We kept moving. Flocks. Herds. Responsibilities." He paused. "And grief. None of us knew how to carry it properly back then."

Joseph lowered his head.

Benjamin stared at the ground, his hand slowly closing around the edge of the water jug. "She gave her life for mine," he said quietly. "All I've ever had of her is that—her death story."

He looked at Joseph. "I've spent my whole life trying to be worthy of that kind of love. But it always felt like a debt I couldn't repay."

Joseph leaned closer and placed a firm hand on his brother's shoulder.

"You were never a debt," he said softly. "You were the light left to us. The reason Father kept walking. The reason I kept hoping."

He paused, eyes searching Benjamin's face.

"We are not what she lost. We are what she gave."

Benjamin blinked, and for a moment, neither of them spoke.

Two sons of Rachel. Still standing. Still walking.

A long silence passed between them.

Then Judah said, "He loved her. You know that."

"I know," Joseph said. "And I wonder if it was too much for him. To love her... and lose her... and then lose me not long after."

"Someday, we will stand by her stone." Joseph said as he turned to face Benjamin.

Departure

By the time they cleaned up and prepared to leave, the morning light had grown stronger. The camp had been cleared, the oxen yoked, and the scouts already sent ahead. Joseph took one last glance toward the cave, where Israel now lay. Then he turned toward the road south, where the old shepherd paths split—one leading home to Egypt, the other curling west toward Bethlehem.

---

1. Rachel's death – Gen 35:16-21

The caravan began to move, slowly at first, then gathering into its rhythm—the long march of sons, soldiers, and memory.

They would not return by the same road. But that made no difference, danger still traveled with them.

Men Planning

The late-morning sky glowed brightly as the caravan moved steadily across the rolling hills of southern Canaan. The clink of bridles, the rhythmic thud of hooves, and the occasional cry of a bird overhead were the only sounds for miles. Dust kicked gently behind the travelers.

Joseph and Benjamin rode side by side, a respectful few paces ahead of the rest of the company, their cloaks flapping lightly in the wind. It had been hours since they spoke, both lost in their thoughts—until Joseph turned with a quiet smile.

"You named your daughter Rachel?"

Benjamin looked over, surprised at the shift in tone. "Of course I did," he said with a soft grin. "It's the only way I could give her back life that she gave up for me."

Joseph nodded slowly.

"Father used to say she looks like her," Benjamin said. "Dark eyes. That same steady gaze, like she's watching everything without a word."

Joseph chuckled. "Dangerous."

"Oh, very," Benjamin smirked. "She keeps her brothers in order. They listen to her more than they do to me sometimes."

Joseph smiled, then his gaze drifted ahead. "About your other daughters..."

Benjamin raised an eyebrow. "You mean the ones you're marrying off to your sons?"

"I mean the ones I hope will find a home with them," Joseph corrected gently. "Ephraim and Manasseh have grown strong, but they need wives who understand both who they are... and who they must become."

Benjamin rubbed his chin. "I've been thinking about that. I have ideas."

"Manasseh... he needs someone who challenges him but also listens to him. He feels deeply. He carries things too long. He gets that from his mother."

Ephraim—he leads like I do. He needs someone steady. Not someone easily overwhelmed by noise or responsibility."

Benjamin laughed. "That rules out two of my youngest, doesn't it?" Then he held up a finger. "Let me not be too quick. One of them already threatened a boy in the courtyard for mocking her tunic color. I think she could tame Manasseh."

Joseph burst out laughing.

"Ephraim will need a wife who sees the long path, not just the next step," Benjamin added.

"But..." Benjamin raised a hand, "I won't make final matches without consulting their mothers. I've learned that lesson."

Joseph barked out a laugh. "That would not go over well. Asenath nearly chased me out of the room when I first brought it up."

Benjamin grinned. "My wives sent me out with figs and a warning not to promise anyone anything until they're asked."

That sent both men into full laughter, loud and warm—the kind that hadn't been heard since the early days of their reconciliation.

Their laughter carried down the caravan line, and soon Judah called out from behind, "What are you two plotting up there? Another treaty between Egypt and the daughters of Benjamin?"

"Just arranging the next generation's headaches," Joseph called back.

Reuben snorted. "Heaven help us."

"Speak for yourself," Zebulun said. "My sons will need wives too. Shall we send word to the Midianites?"

Issachar leaned over to Naphtali. "I'll take a Midianite over one of Benjamin's little generals. I've seen them fight over figs."

Even Simeon, usually quiet, smirked. "Let them marry. Then let's see who actually rules."

The whole caravan rippled with chuckles, easing the weight of the road. For a moment, the brothers were simply that—brothers again, sharing the absurdities and affections of life.

At the Rear

Meanwhile, Ephraim and Manasseh rode near the back, flanked by two mounted guards and a small group of attendants. The dust of the road clung to their boots and cloaks. The distance from the front irritated them more than the ride itself.

Manasseh shifted in his saddle, eyes narrowed. "What are they laughing about now?"

Ephraim huffed. "Probably planning our futures without us."

"I hate this," Manasseh muttered. "Like we're children being hidden from the firelight."

He nudged his mount forward. But the guard on his right reached out with his staff, barring the horse with a firm but respectful tap.

"Your father asked that you remain toward the rear until we cross into Egyptian patrol lands."

Manasseh glared. "We're not children."

"No, sir," the guard replied calmly. "But we're not taking chances."

"They're not just Pharaoh's men," Ephraim added quietly. "They're loyal to Father. They'd lay down their lives for him—without question."

Manasseh followed his brother's gaze, his frown softening.

"That's why we stay back," Ephraim said. "Not because we're weak. Because they won't risk losing us."

Ephraim's gaze drifted to the guards flanking them, watching with practiced ease.

He tugged at Manasseh's reins, holding his brother back. "Let it go. For now."

Manasseh scowled but obeyed. "It's just... they're planning our marriages up there, I can feel it."

Ephraim smirked faintly. "They're our uncles. They probably think they're doing us a favor."

Manasseh frowned.

And still, they rode on.

Unseen Watcher

Golden light slipped behind the western hills, casting long shadows across the caravan as it wound its way through the lower passes. Laughter still echoed from the front where Joseph and his brothers rode, and the dust of the road curled upward in lazy plumes.

Far from the noise, the two spies sat crouched behind a rocky outcrop, positioned slightly uphill and overlooking the caravan's trail. They had paused behind the caravan, pretending to tighten saddle gear and check their packs. Now they watched—carefully.

"They've let their guard down," the younger spy murmured. "Did you hear that laughter?"

The elder nodded slowly, eyes locked on Joseph. "They think the worst is behind them. That the mourning is over."

The younger fingered the edge of his cloak. "And those two sons... kept at the rear like cargo. They'll be exposed soon enough. If we strike during camp, we can finish it before anyone draws a blade."

"No," the elder said, voice calm. "We strike when they least expect it, when Joseph is off alone. When the light fades but before the stars are clear."

He pulled a small bronze ring from his pouch; its crest bearing the hidden seal of Amun's inner circle. "The priesthood watches for our return. If we fail, they will bury us deeper than the Hebrew tombs."

The younger frowned. "Then we don't fail."

They watched again in silence.

Ahead of them, Joseph was still laughing, his shoulders shaking with warmth, his hand brushing his horse's mane as he joked with Benjamin. His brothers leaned in close, teasing and loud and full of life.

The elder spy sneered. "He's forgotten the pit. Let's remind him."

Unbeknownst to them, they were not alone.

High above, nestled in the cleft of a narrow slope shaded by a cluster of thornbush and stone, Dan lay still, pressed low, wrapped in a weathered cloak the color of dust.

He had broken away from the main group hours ago, slipping into the wilderness under the pretense of checking a water route. No one had followed. With so many officials, guards, and servants moving within the caravan, his absence remained unnoticed.

Except to Joseph. He had seen the flicker of Dan's movement and had given the slightest nod.

Now, Dan watched.

He couldn't hear their words, but he saw their posture, the way they crouched too low, the way they didn't relax like travelers at rest. He noticed how their eyes remained too focused on Joseph; their movements were too controlled.

They weren't pilgrims. They weren't mourners.

He counted the distance. He marked the wind. He kept still.

Later, he would circle back toward Joseph's tent under the cover of dusk and report his observations.

For now, he watched the watchers.

And he waited.

Moving Closer

The snap of wood echoed through the hills like a cracking whip. One of the rear carts buckled against a stone buried in the dirt path, its wheel breaking sharply to one side. Supplies spilled. A clay jar shattered. Dust rose in a cloud.

Cries went up. Guards moved quickly to assist.

Two men, unassuming in their tan robes, were among the first to respond.

The temple spies.

They moved with trained ease, lifting bundles, offering advice. One of them examined the wheel, pointing to the axle. "Lift here," he instructed. "The angle's off—it must be wedged before the wheel can be replaced."

The guards welcomed their help. No one questioned them. They were scribes, after all—part of Pharaoh's entourage.

But the two men weren't watching the cart.

They were watching Ephraim and Manasseh.

The boys sat nearby, momentarily unguarded as the soldiers focused on the broken cart. Manasseh had dismounted and was watching the repairs with open curiosity. Ephraim leaned against a tree, arms crossed.

"They're never far from him," the younger spy said under his breath.

"We strike when they are," the elder replied.

Neither knew they had been marked in return.

The Servant and the Spring

Just as the sun dipped low, Benjamin walked alone to draw water, beyond the edge of the camp. The spring ran quietly beneath an overhang, and a line of clay jugs waited to be filled.

He was crouching, arms wet to the elbows, when a young servant stepped up beside him, carrying a tall water jug. Thin, sharp-eyed, no more than thirteen years old.

"May I help, my lord?" the boy asked, kneeling beside him.

Benjamin glanced sideways. "I don't know your face."

"I'm with Lord Ayar's caravan," the servant replied. "But... not truly."

He leaned closer. "My grandfather once served Pharaoh. He was in prison a long time ago. A Hebrew man interpreted his dream—and saved his life."

Benjamin's heartbeat slowed. "The butler?" he asked calmly.

The young man nodded.

"Who are you? And why are you telling me this now?"

"My name is Zamar. My grandfather, Rahkim, told me *If you ever find the man I speak of, serve him. Protect him. He serves a God who sees everything.*"

Zamar glanced back toward the tents. "There's a plan to kill him—Joseph, from my master, Lord Ayar. He blames him for Egypt's refusal of trade. He said once the body is in the cave, Joseph's blood will flow."

A chill rippled through Benjamin's chest. His hand slipped slightly on the jug's rim, water sloshing over his fingers. He steadied it, masking the flood of panic that went through his body.

Zamar added, "He travels with armed men. They won't strike with blades drawn. They'll wait for silence. They'll make it look like an accident... or a message."

Benjamin's face tightened.

"You've done well," he said. "Go. Tell no one else. Not even those you trust."

Zamar disappeared back into the night.

Benjamin stood alone by the water, jug half-filled, pulse racing.

He had to move quickly.

The Inner Circle Forms

Joseph stood near the fire, hands clasped behind his back, speaking quietly with Amennakht when Benjamin appeared, face grim.

"I need a word," he said.

Joseph followed him to the edge of camp, where the shadows cloaked them in quiet.

Benjamin relayed the warning in full. When he finished, Joseph's face was concerned.

"You trust the servant's warning?" Benjamin asked

"I do. Rahkim was the butler. I remember. Plus, Elohim would not leave us unaware."

Joseph did remember it all: the face, the dreams, the sudden freedom.

He exhaled. "Then it's worse than we thought. Two threats. Neither aware of the other."

"Two threats? Who is behind the other threat?" Benjamin could hardly believe the turn of events.

"High Priest Nefer-Ra most likely. They have been trying to kill me from the moment I took office."

He thought for a moment, then nodded slowly. "Bring Naphtali, Judah, and Zebulun. Dan is already watching. I'll call him in when we move."

Benjamin hesitated. "Not Levi?"

"Not yet," Joseph said carefully. "He strikes too quickly. I need a clear head first."

Benjamin agreed.

Within the hour, they were gathered in Joseph's tent. Quiet men, quick minds, strong hands. They listened in silence as Joseph relayed both threats—the temple spies, and now Lord Ayar's assassins.

"Two groups," he said, his voice steady. "They plan to strike when we least expect it. We will turn that against them."

Judah's mouth curled. "Divide them?"

"Divide and observe," Joseph nodded. "And when the time comes—choose which falls first."

Outside, the stars shimmered coldly in the sky.

The caravan rested.

But the sons of Israel were awake.

And now, they were ready.

Chapter Twelve

THE WOMEN WHO REMEMBER

The Library

The soft scratching of reed against parchment filled the chamber.

Asenath sat at a long stone table beneath the western colonnade of the estate, the early light filtering through woven curtains. Scrolls lay half-unrolled across the surface—lists of grain distribution during the famine, reports from district governors, and her careful notes in clean, practiced script.

Her hand moved deliberately, notating a scroll titled: *On the Preservation of Egypt in the Days of Famine.* But the rhythm of her writing slowed every so often, her eyes drifting to the horizon.

It had been many days. Longer than expected.

She wouldn't say she was afraid. But the waiting, the silence—it unsettled her.

Footsteps approached. A palace guard, out of breath from the road, entered the courtyard and bowed deeply.

"My lady, a message from the court," he said. "The caravan is nearing the edge of the eastern territories. Four days' journey from home. All is well."

As the guard's footsteps retreated, Asenath remained still. The silence enveloped her like a memory.

The last time Joseph had left Egypt, it had been a perilous experience—both politically and personally. The weight of Pharaoh's favor didn't always shield him from jealousy or whispers.

She had taken the boys and stayed in On with her brother during that time, watching the palace from afar, wondering if Joseph would return safely—or at all.

Now, as she rose to gather the scrolls, her decision to visit her family that afternoon felt like a quiet ritual of its own—a mirror of old anxieties, laced with hope.

An Afternoon Visit

That afternoon, Asenath chose simple elegance—light linen robes without adornment and a soft veil to guard against the sun. At her quiet request that morning, a servant had arranged for her chariot to wait at the estate gate, flanked by two discreet guards bearing no crest, but loyal to Joseph's house.

She stepped into the chariot with practiced ease, offering a nod to the driver. The city streets were alive with motion—vendors shouting prices, children darting between carts, oxen shifting under the weight of woven goods. Her presence drew a few admiring glances, but no fanfare followed. She preferred it that way.

By the time they reached her family's home in the temple quarter, the guards had dismounted to announce her. Her father—once the High Priest of On—greeted her at the threshold with his usual blend of reverence and restraint. Her mother embraced her lightly, while her cousins and aunts gathered on the shaded balcony.

Pomegranate wine was poured, the scent of sweet resin and baked barley drifting through the air. Hours passed in quiet conversation, the breeze stirring robes and memory alike.

Conversation turned—as it often did—to Ephraim and Manasseh.

"Ephraim must be near his twenty-second year," her aunt said, refilling a cup. "Surely it's time to discuss a bride."

"There are well-bred girls in On," her mother added. "They know how to carry a household and stand at court. Highborn. Respectable."

Her father nodded thoughtfully. "Sons of a Vizier—and a priest's daughter—should have wives that reflect their rank."

Asenath offered a polite smile but didn't answer right away.

After a pause, she set down her cup and rose gently to her feet. "Forgive me, I must return. I have a meeting at the estate."

"Oh?" her mother asked. "Another function?"

"Something quieter," Asenath said smoothly. "Joseph and I, along with Dinah, are building a small library. A private archive. We're preserving the accounts of the famine, the Hebrews' contribution to Egypt, and other records that may be helpful in the years to come."

Her father's eyes narrowed with curiosity. "You're using your scribal training?"

Asenath nodded. "At last."

There was a pause—brief but weighted. Then her father stepped closer, resting a hand lightly on her shoulder. "You always had the best hand," he said. "Even as a girl, you could balance elegance with precision. I trained many scribes, but few wrote with the clarity of mind and purpose that you did."

Asenath looked up at him, surprised by the softness in his voice.

He added, "I had wondered if Egypt would ever see the fruit of it."

Her mother smiled gently. "And now it is bearing fruit in a new way."

"It is," Asenath said. "We're writing down what would otherwise be lost—the memories, the moments that aren't in ledgers or temple walls."

Her mother stepped forward and took her hand. "Then it is good work. The kind that outlives empires. May the gods bless your efforts... and may your children know what you've built."

Asenath bowed her head, a small smile tugging at the corners of her mouth. "That's why we do it."

She offered a few more courteous goodbyes, then stepped into the sunlit courtyard, her pace steady but swift.

At the gate, she nodded to the servant holding it open. Her guards—two men in discreet linen livery—fell into step behind her as she crossed the narrow street and into the waiting chariot. The driver snapped the reins, and the horses moved forward.

She allowed herself a small, silent laugh. She had escaped another round of matchmaking.

And more importantly, the work waited.

The truth still had to be written.

Making Bread

In a modest home nestled near the palace wall, laughter danced through the rooms, soft and warm as rising bread. Dinah stood at the clay counter, her sleeves rolled high, hands dusted with flour, her mind focused—not just on the task, but on the memory.

Beside her, Nari and Kiya tried to mimic every move, their tiny hands clumsy but eager. A woven cloth protected the lentil pot simmering nearby, its aroma mingling with garlic, cumin, and something older—something sacred.

"Not like that, Kiya," Dinah said gently, catching the girl's wrist before she pressed too hard. "You fold the edge, then turn it over. One movement, like you're wrapping a promise."

Kiya giggled, trying again. Nari stood on tiptoes, intently watching Dinah's face.

"What are you thinking about?" Nari asked.

Dinah didn't answer right away. She was watching her fingers, retracing each motion as if it were a prayer. The right measure of water. The exact moment the dough softened. The sound of bubbling lentils when the fire was just right. The rhythm mattered.

She was remembering-not for herself, but for the scribe.

Asenath had asked her to teach the archivists what it meant to live as a Hebrew woman—how the hands remembered when the scrolls could not. Dinah could not write. But she could speak the past into permanence.

She moved slowly now, speaking under her breath.

"This was my mother's way," she murmured. "Leah said the bread should be folded once for the heart, once for the tent, and once for the road."

Nari blinked. "Three folds?"

Dinah nodded. "Always."

She glanced at the pot. "And lentils for mourning, but also for healing. Because life keeps moving."

She didn't explain the full weight of those words. Not yet.

Outside, the streets of Egypt bustled—merchants shouting, oxen braying, the low hum of courtly life carrying on as if nothing else existed outside their borders.

But inside this small kitchen, a woman once forgotten was preserving her people—not with parchment and reed, but with memory, flour, and heart.

She would visit Asenath tomorrow and sit with the scribe in the quiet room beside the fountain.

And she would speak these moments aloud, so they could be remembered—for the ones who would one day leave Egypt carrying more than gold.

They would carry the story.

They would carry faith.

They would carry her.

In the Temple Shadows

Far from the pleasant smells of Dinah's kitchen, within the deepest chamber of the temple of Amun, the air was heavy with incense and secrecy.

Six High Priests stood in a perfect circle, their linen robes etched with sacred markings, their faces hidden deep within their oversized hoods.

In the center of the floor, a basin of water reflected one flame (but there were no candles in the room).

An obsidian knife lay beside it.

The High Priest, Nefer-Ra, lifted both hands. His voice was low, rhythmic, ancient.

"We call upon Heka, god of magic. We call upon Sekhmet, the destroyer. May the path of the usurper be broken."

They poured oil onto burning coals. A hiss of smoke rose.

"We bind his steps," chanted another. "Let his feet falter. Let the arrow find his back. Let the god who raised him fall silent."

They circled the basin once, each dipping their fingers and drawing a mark upon the stone floor.

Nefer-Ra's oldest son spoke hesitantly. "And if he returns unharmed?"

The High Priest answered without turning. "Then we try again. Until the body of Joseph is dust."

As he spoke, his hand moved instinctively to the gold amulet at his chest—an ancient symbol of Heka, carved with runes no longer spoken aloud. It pulsed with a faint heat, its surface shimmering faintly.

The water in the basin rippled—not with wind, but with force, spreading in rings that defied the stillness of the air. Nefer-Ra's son stepped back.

Nefer-Ra's voice deepened. "He was raised by a god not our own. Let him fall by one he cannot name."

The oil hissed. The shadows lengthened.

And still, they chanted.

Chapter Thirteen

The Ambush

Evil Moves

The sun hovered low in the sky. The road ahead narrowed into a pass between low stone ridges and scraggly trees—a forgotten shepherd's trail Joseph had chosen intentionally.

The perfect place for a trap. Or an ambush.

The caravan slowed, its pace gentle but steady. Everything looked routine: carts groaning under their weight, servants murmuring to one another, animals braying with fatigue. Dust curled in the air, lazily caught by the wind. The scent of sweat and leather lingered.

But within the caravan, everything had shifted.

Ephraim and Manasseh, usually at the rear, now rode near the front, flanked by two seasoned guards. The brothers' expressions were controlled, though Manasseh's fingers tapped anxiously on the reins.

Behind them, Joseph rode beside Benjamin, posture casual, voice low. Just ahead of them, Judah and Zebulun had slowed slightly, scanning the cliffs without appearing to do so.

To far side of the trail, Naphtali had slipped into the brush, silent as a fox, ready to circle from above.

Dan was already gone—vanished the night before to watch the ridge from its far side. If any threat rose behind them, he would be the first to see it.

Near the rear of the line, the two temple spies broke off again, offering to scout ahead for better footing.

"No need to strain the oxen," one said. "We'll mark any holes or erosion in the path."

They were granted space without suspicion.

They blended easily into the flow. But their eyes were locked on Joseph. And on his sons.

"We strike when the dust rises again," the elder whispered. "When they're distracted. The sound will cover the blade."

"They won't see it coming," the younger murmured.

The Second Threat

On the far side of the ridge, another danger stirred.

Three men from Lord Ayar's retinue crouched low in a shallow hollow, their backs pressed against the stone, watching the procession like hawks circling prey. Their sandals shifted on loose shale, one nearly tumbling before he steadied himself.

"That's him," one muttered, pointing toward the figure in the red sash, just behind the sons at the front. "Next to the dark horse. That's Joseph."

"Wait until he clears the bend. Isolate him from the rear guard."

A third man, younger, more hesitant, crouched farther back. "Are we sure it must be today? So close to Egypt?"

"The order was clear. No return. No hesitation."

They tightened their grip on curved blades—simple weapons made for quick work and easy escape.

None of them saw Dan watching from above.

None of them knew another threat was already unraveling.

The path narrowed.

The rocky bend ahead twisted between rising ridges and scrub trees, perfect for shade—and shadows.

Behind them, the slanting sun sharpened every edge in gold, turning brush and stone into twitching silhouettes.

Silent Alarm

Ephraim felt it first. Not the click of the stone. Not the signal. But the stillness.

The kind of silence the desert made just before something snapped.

Dust spiraled around their horses' hooves in lazy curls. The slope to their left seemed ordinary—stone, thorn, dry brush—but his skin tingled—the way it used to before a storm.

He glanced sideways at Manasseh, who was fidgeting again—his fingers tapping the saddle, jaw set tight.

"This doesn't feel right," Ephraim muttered.

Manasseh didn't hesitate. "Something's happening."

They had been moved forward that morning, told it was a shift in the formation routine, safer, and less dusty. But too many glances, too many stiff nods. Their uncles rode just a little too far apart. Everything looked normal—until you looked closely.

Ephraim looked behind him—a guard had drifted forward, placing himself between them and the curve behind.

"Did Father tell you anything?" Manasseh asked under his breath.

"No," Ephraim answered. "You?"

Manasseh shook his head. "He's keeping us out of something."

"That's the part that bothers me," Ephraim said. "He wouldn't do that... unless he had to."

Ephraim scanned the slope again. He caught a glimmer—a movement where there shouldn't have been one. A shape in the brush, gone too quickly to name.

He leaned in close. "Do you think we're the target?"

"I think we're the bait," Manasseh replied quietly.

Judah spotted it—a glint too clean beneath a traveler's cloak, the rigid spine of a man who had once moved as loose as rope. He shifted in his saddle: forward, left, forward again.

The signal was given.

Zebulun responded instantly, narrowing the space behind Ephraim and Manasseh.

Naphtali still moving along the brush, silent as breath.

From above, Dan's stone dropped—click—a whisper of warning striking rock just behind Joseph's mount.

The trap was set.

Joseph leaned forward in his saddle, gaze steady.

The stone had spoken. Naphtali's cloth flicked once in the breeze.

Without turning, Joseph gave the word—soft, calculated...

"Now."

Judah surged.

Zebulun cut left.

The trap snapped shut.

The Ambush Spoiled

It began as a whisper in the dust—then the sound of feet skidding on loose stone.

From the left ridge, Ayar's first assassin leapt, blade gleaming in the light, his target unmistakable: Joseph.

But Joseph was already turning. The blade arced—Judah intercepted it with his leather-wrapped forearm, twisting mid-swing and slamming the assassin to the ground with a thud that shattered the silence.

A second attacker rushed in from behind, aiming for Ephraim.

Zebulun tackled him to the ground, sending both men crashing into the scrub brush. Ephraim wheeled his horse back and shouted, "Stay down!" to Manasseh, who had drawn his blade but hadn't yet moved.

Naphtali burst from the shadows, striking the third assassin with a sweep of his staff to the knees, then spun the weapon once and drove the butt into the man's ribs. The attacker folded, groaning.

Joseph dismounted in one fluid motion.

He stood over the first would-be killer, breathing hard. "Ayar should have sent better men."

The assassin spat dust and blood, eyes wide with disbelief.

Benjamin arrived seconds later, flanked by two guards. "All three down?"

Judah wiped his arm. "Sloppy and loud. Must have thought we were still grieving."

Joseph gave a single nod. "Take them alive. We'll let Pharaoh decide what to do with Ayar's diplomacy."

Too Late

Further back in the caravan, the two temple spies had watched everything.

Hidden behind the broken cart they had used to reposition earlier, the younger one whispered, "Now's the moment—they're distracted."

"They'll be winded. Disorganized," the elder said, gripping his dagger.

He rose slowly, moving with purpose, his eyes locked on Manasseh, now circling back toward his father.

The younger slipped between carts, moving silently toward Ephraim.

But they hadn't seen Dan.

He emerged from the far ridge with a silent leap, landing like a falling shadow behind the younger spy.

Dan didn't shout.

He didn't warn.

He simply moved.

A flash of steel—one silent motion—and the younger man fell, his breath snatched away before it could become a scream.

The elder turned too late, his dagger half-raised when Naphtali stepped behind him, staff extended. He swept the man's legs, and Dan finished the job.

Two bodies lay still in the dirt.

Fear and Awe

The dust in the air hung like a curtain, suspended in the golden light of late afternoon.

Around the clearing, the caravan was frozen — dozens of servants, guards, officials, and bystanders stunned into stillness. Even the animals stood quiet, sensing something sacred had passed through the space.

Ephraim and Manasseh stood motionless.

They stared down at the two lifeless men—strangers who had ridden with them for days, silent, watchful. Dangerous.

Manasseh swallowed hard. "I didn't see it coming."

Ephraim nodded, his throat dry. "Neither did they."

He looked at Dan, still standing near the bodies with calm, measured breath, and then at Zebulun wiping blood from his sleeve, Judah adjusting his knife, Naphtali watching the ridgeline with cold precision.

They were shepherds. But they were also something else.

Warriors.

Manasseh stepped closer to his father, voice low. "Did you always know they could do this?"

Joseph glanced at his sons, "I knew they'd protect what matters," he said with quiet pride. "That's enough."

Reuben stepped forward, eyes wide. "There were two groups."

Levi, gripping his staff tighter than he needed to, muttered, "And we never saw either of them."

Simeon looked at Joseph. "How did you—?"

"I listened," Joseph said. "To Dan. To Elohim. To my gut."

Benjamin exhaled, still flushed from the fight. "And to your sons. They felt it too."

Judah smiled grimly. "They are learning."

"They're learning now," Joseph said, eyes locked on Ephraim and Manasseh. "Like we all did."

Behind them, Amennakht rode up at last, flanked by Pharaoh's elite escort. Their blades were drawn, though unused.

"Too late," one of them muttered.

"They were handled," Joseph said.

The captain surveyed the bodies, the bound prisoners, the stunned silence. He gave a slight nod, respectful. "We'll take the prisoners from here. Pharaoh will want the truth."

"And the bodies?" Judah asked.

Amennakht signaled. Four soldiers dismounted. Two went for the temple spies. Two for the men from Ayar's camp. No ceremony—just swift removal.The captain paused, eyes sweeping over the scene one last time. Then, under his breath, he murmured a brief invocation in Egyptian:"May Ma'at witness justice. May the scales remain balanced."He nodded once to Joseph, the unspoken bond of respect passing between them.

"Let Egypt see what happens when it forgets who saved it. Praise be to Elohim," Joseph said quietly.

A Thunderous Praise

And then, as if some invisible line had snapped, Simeon lifted his voice.

A single phrase, ancient and familiar, rising like a battle cry and a prayer at once.

"Blessed be the name of Elohim, who delivers His people!"

Judah repeated it. Then Levi. Then Zebulun.

The others joined. The caravan roared.

"Blessed be the name of Elohim, who delivers His people!"

Voices rang out across stone and sky, echoing through the hills and shaking the dust off every soul who heard them.

Ephraim and Manasseh shouted too, not because they understood everything, but because they believed it.

Chapter Fourteen

The Return Home

The End of the Journey

Golden light spilled across the city rooftops as the caravan rolled through the gates of the Vizier's estate. The outer walls of Joseph's home shimmered softly, glowing with the welcoming warmth of homecoming. Servants lined the courtyard, welcoming them with water, fresh cloths to wipe away the dust, and trays of food.

The air was thick with laughter, embraces, and the scent of roasted garlic and wine-soaked lamb.

Brothers who had once fought like wolves now embraced like sons of peace. Cloaks were unfastened, dust was shaken off, and stories—already exaggerated—began to take shape.

"I told you we were being watched!" Manasseh declared, waving a piece of bread for emphasis.

"Not before I told you," Ephraim grinned, elbowing him.

"Don't let them fool you," Zebulun said, pointing at them. "They wanted to run back to Egypt before the blades even left their sheaths."

Laughter erupted.

Simeon stretched his back with a groan. "All I know is that if we had to fight one more priest, I'd start charging a fee."

Levi rolled his eyes. "As if anyone would pay to see you fight."

"I'd pay," Naphtali said. "Just to see how fast he'd lose."

Reuben leaned into a pillar, half-laughing, half-weeping. "I've missed my children. My wife. Even the goats."

Judah gave a wide grin. "I miss a proper meal and a bed that doesn't creak like camel bones."

The crowd chuckled again. And amid it all, Dinah stood with Nari and Kiya, offering smiles and blessings, welcoming her brothers home with plates of warm bread and lentils.

Welcome Home

At the entrance to the house, Asenath stood in the doorway, wrapped in a soft white shawl, her hands clasped in front of her. She said nothing at first—just watched.

Her boys saw her first.

Ephraim and Manasseh broke away from the group, grinning, dirty, and still smelling faintly of horses and road dust. But they ran to her, as if they were children again, throwing their arms around her waist.

She laughed softly, tears in her eyes as she embraced them.

"You're too tall for this," she murmured.

"You're never too tall to hug your mother," Ephraim whispered.

They stepped back, still clasping her hands, and then, without another word, rushed toward the kitchens.

"Food!" Manasseh called. "Real food!"

"Save some for the rest of us!" Benjamin shouted behind them.

Joseph remained at the edge of the courtyard, saying a final word to Amennakht, shaking hands with the guards, and giving blessings to the servants and helpers.

Only when the last guest had passed through the gate did he turn.

Asenath was still waiting.

He walked to her slowly, dust on his boots, cloak slung loosely over one shoulder. Joseph exhaled, a long breath he hadn't realized he'd been holding for days.

Their eyes met, and for a moment, they said nothing.

Then Asenath smiled, tilting her head.

"Well?" she asked. "Are you going to tell me about it? Or do I need to get the boys to act it out for me?"

Joseph stepped into the doorway, took her hands in his, and smiled.

"Let me wash off the road... and everything that nearly happened on it."

She leaned forward, pressing her forehead to his.

"I'm not going anywhere."

Joseph washed and changed, then made his way to the kitchen, where laughter, clinking cups, and the clatter of feet and forks filled the air.

He was home.

The Village Square

Word of the caravan's return had spread quickly beyond the estate walls. By late afternoon, the center of the village was alive with motion. Children darted between olive trees and clay walls, chasing each other with shouts and shrill laughter. Vendors reappeared, setting out baskets of early figs and pressed cheese, hoping to catch returning servants with coin to spare.

At the center of the square, the brothers gathered again—no longer soldiers or scouts, but men at ease.

They found themselves leaning against walls, sitting on overturned baskets, sharing wine from clay pitchers passed hand to hand.

Judah, recounting the ambush with exaggerated flair, slapped his thigh. "The assassin leapt down, right? And Joseph just..." he made a slow motion, mimicking a cloak swirl and a perfect sidestep, "like a breeze moving out of his way!"

Reuben groaned. "He did not. It was Judah who nearly fell off his horse trying to turn too fast!"

Benjamin raised both hands. "Enough! No one remembers it right but me."

"Of course not," Zebulun grinned. "The baby son of Rachel and the hero of every tale."

"That reminds me," Naphtali said with a sly look, "how many daughters do you have now, Benjamin?"

"Too many to count," Levi muttered. "And every one of them louder than the last."

"Ephraim and Manasseh will have their hands full," Simeon added. "If you let them choose, that is."

At this, Benjamin's smile faltered slightly. He turned just in time to see his wife across the square—arms folded, eyebrow raised.

A burst of laughter followed.

Judah clapped him on the back. "You'll be lucky if she lets you into your own house tonight."

"I'm sleeping in the barn," Benjamin mumbled, and everyone howled again.

Resting at Last

One by one, the brothers began to peel away, called by children with wild hair and dirt-streaked cheeks, by wives with raised brows and open arms. They disappeared into doorways and courtyards, into circles of firelight and fresh linens, into laughter and familiar hands.

In the center of the village, stories spilled from mouths faster than the bread could be passed. Judah mimed a sword fight with a broomstick. Zebulun shouted over him, claiming he had taken down the first assassin. Benjamin, blushing, tried to hush his brothers as they teased him about matchmaking and his daughters' fierce tempers.

"Savta Zilpah would have scolded us for less," someone muttered through a laugh.

"She probably still will," Reuben said, turning toward the edge of the gathering.

And there she was.

Zilpah stood quietly near the place where Israel's tent had once stood. Since their departure to Hebron, she had seen to it all—folded his garments, whispered one last blessing over his sleeping mat, and supervised the respectful dismantling of the tent. It was no longer a place of mourning. It was a space made ready for memory—and for belonging.

She waited with her hands clasped before her, shoulders wrapped in a simple shawl. Not as a servant. Not even as a concubine.

Just a mother.

Gad was the first to reach her, slowing as he drew near. One of his youngest rushed forward with a squeal, flinging small arms around her waist.

"Savta!" the child cried.

Zilpah bent slowly, her joints stiff, but her embrace warm and certain. "I thought you'd forgotten your old Savta," she murmured, brushing dust from the child's cheek.

"Never," said one of the older ones, hovering just behind.

"Did you bring us stories?" another asked, eyes bright.

Zilpah smiled. "Only the ones that matter. The ones your grandfather told me, when none of you were born yet."

Gad stepped beside her and offered his arm. "Come, Savta. The room is ready."

Zilpah laid her hand on his. "And the bread?"

"Still warm," his wife called from inside.

Zilpah nodded. "Then I'm home."

As twilight descended, the last of the sons of Israel made their way inside. Laughter still streamed across the courtyards. Smoke curled from bread ovens. Children danced barefoot through the dust. Elders leaned close, trading memories over dates and warm lentils.

And in the middle of it all, beneath stars that had once watched over Abraham's wandering steps and Jacob's long nights, the house of Israel lived on—loud, imperfect, beloved.

As night deepened, the torches were lit—soft halos of light dotting doorways and alleyways, casting gentle shadows on stone.

Fires crackled. Doors opened and closed. Laughter moved like music across rooftops and walkways. Somewhere, a flute played. Somewhere else, a lullaby rose over the cries of children. And everywhere, there was the sense of something returned. Of something right.

The patriarch had been laid to rest with his fathers.

The sons of Israel had come home. Not just to a house. But to one another.

To shared memory.

To story.

To promise.

And in every window and tent, in every small kitchen and crowded room, the name of Elohim lingered on grateful lips.

A Reckoning Begins

At the palace in Memphis, Pharaoh sat beneath the gilded canopy of judgment, his body language unreadable as Amennakht knelt before him, recounting every detail—the burial, the ambush, the spies from the temple, and the assassins tied to Lord Ayar.

When Amennakht finished, silence settled like a cloud of smoke.

Pharaoh's fingers drummed once on the arm of his throne. Then he spoke with eyes full of wrath.

"Summon Nefer-Ra."

The command echoed down the marble hall, and servants scattered like startled birds.

In the deepest chamber beneath the palace—a place few dared to enter—torches flickered as if they too were scared.

The High Priest of Amun, robed in shadow and pride, was being summoned.

Not for counsel.

But for reckoning.

Chapter Fifteen

JOSEPH'S LEGACY

The Library of Remembrance

The courtyard of Joseph's estate glowed beneath a canopy of woven reeds, the sun softened into golden beams that filtered down onto linen-covered tables and stone benches. Beneath it, scrolls lay unfurled on stone benches and linen-covered tables. The scent of papyrus and myrrh drifted through the air, mingling with the sound of reeds scratching across parchment.

Asenath moved slowly through the scriptorium, sorting through baskets of scrolls. Her fingers paused over a worn manuscript; the ink had faded, but the message was clear. She handed it to Dinah, who was collecting a pile of scrolls to be written.

Asenath said softly, "There will come a time when our children ask who they are. They must have more than memories—they must have truth written in their own hand."

Dinah looked at the pile of scrolls in her arms, her eyes steady. "And what we dared not forget."

On the far side of the courtyard, Ephraim oversaw the careful cataloging of materials. He moved among the scroll keepers, ensuring that every piece of family wisdom, every historical record, every memory of the patriarchs was being preserved.

Manasseh stood at the entrance, arms crossed, speaking quietly with traders and artisans who had brought more ink and tools. He ensured the guards rotated shifts, maintaining quiet vigilance to safeguard the project.

A few of the brothers' wives sat together under an olive tree, murmuring as they contributed what they could: birth stories, migration routes, sacred songs remembered from Jacob's tent.

In a separate gathering that afternoon in Goshen, Joseph met with his brothers. They sat in a circle, their eyes turned toward the aging Vizier.

"We cannot leave our children ignorant," Joseph began. "We must teach them. To write. To read. To know who they are and whose they are."

Judah nodded slowly. "Not just our stories. But how to build. How to govern."

"They must be more than shepherds," Joseph continued. "They must be thinkers, scribes, merchants, advisors. Let every village have a school. Let every child be counted."

The brothers nodded in agreement without hesitation.

Joseph and Asenath would fund the first school near the central marketplace in Goshen, and Ephraim and Manasseh pledged to pay the first year of the instructors' salaries. The plan was clear: literacy would strengthen the people, and education would ensure their future.

Back at the estate, Asenath continued to oversee the scriptorium. Joseph's vision, once born in dreams, was now unfolding in scroll and stone.

The next evening, as the stars emerged over the estate, Joseph and Asenath sat outside alone beneath a flowering fig tree. The soft chirping of crickets filled the quiet space between them.

They had both recently returned from Goshen and had taken time to observe the daughters of Benjamin—bright, modest, and full of grace.

Joseph broke the silence. "I've watched them at the gatherings, in the gardens, even at the school. Two stand apart. They carry themselves with wisdom beyond their years."

Asenath nodded slowly. "The eldest, Rachel, is steady and thoughtful. And the younger, Tirzah, has a quiet strength. I saw her calm a quarrel among the children without raising her voice."

Joseph smiled. "Ephraim respects her. He said she listens like a counselor and speaks like a leader."

"And Manasseh has already started helping Rachel with the scrolls," Asenath added with a knowing look. "He lingers longer each time."

They shared a glance, the understanding between them unspoken.

"If they are willing," Joseph said, "let us begin preparations."

Asenath placed her hand over his. "Then it will be a double wedding—and a blessing for us all."

The Decision

A few nights later, as the sun dipped low over the Nile, the brothers gathered on the upper terrace of Joseph's estate. Jasmine clung to the walls. The river shimmered in the distance, and the scent of figs hung on the breeze as they reclined on cushions around a low table.

The mood was easy—laughter echoing under the open sky, voices raised in teasing and stories of old.

Benjamin leaned toward Joseph, his tone shifting to one that was more earnest. "You've seen them, haven't you? Rachel and Tirzah?"

Joseph nodded. "I have. They are more than daughters, Benjamin. They are women of discernment."

Reuben chuckled, "They take after their mother—thank Elohim."

The group laughed.

Judah raised his goblet. "I saw Tirzah silence Zebulun's grandson with a glance last week. That child hasn't misbehaved since."

Issachar grinned, "And Rachel has read more scrolls than my sons. She's too clever for any one man—except maybe Manasseh."

Benjamin's smile softened. "They've grown into something far beyond what I imagined. When I saw Manasseh helping Rachel gather the scrolls, and Ephraim lingering near Tirzah... I knew."

Joseph turned to him. "And you approve?"

Benjamin looked around at the circle of weathered, laughing faces. "I do. With all my heart."

Zebulun clapped his hands. "Then it's settled. A double wedding!"

Cheers rose, cups lifted. The brothers toasted not just to union, but to legacy, to joy, and the strength of family renewed.

Joseph sat back, eyes shining, the sound of his brothers' laughter echoing around him. For a moment, it felt like Eden.

At the edge of the courtyard, just beyond the glow of the torchlight, Asenath stood quietly, a shawl drawn over her shoulders. She watched the brothers laugh and speak with one another, Joseph among them, not as Vizier, but as brother and friend. Her heart swelled with love.

And yet, a question lingered.

How will I explain this to my family? she wondered. Two of her sons are marrying daughters from Goshen. Not noblewomen of On, not daughters of priests or scribes—but daughters of Hebrew shepherds.

Still, as she thought about Ephraim's face when Tirzah's name was spoken, and Manasseh's shy glance when Rachel's was mentioned, she saw something more profound than tradition. She saw purpose. And hope.

She turned away, silently preparing for what would come next.

A Garden Brings Opportunity

At the same time, far on the other side of Pharoah's palace, Dinah sat with Horem beneath the trellis of their home. This side of the city was clustered with small neighborhoods, mostly people who worked in the palace and the market place. Horem was threading a new spool into his palm-sized sewing frame and she was braiding her hair. A small lamp between them.

Horem cleared his throat, voice low and thoughtful. "One of the traders passed word today that there's an opening in the palace kitchen garden."

Dinah paused, fingers stilling. "The one near the queen's quarters?"

He nodded. "The steward says they need someone to oversee the herbs and root cellar. Nothing grand. But steady work. Quiet. Trusted."

Dinah's lips curved into a knowing smile, though she kept her gaze on the lamp. "I'd have to leave before dawn."

"You would," he said. "But you'd be back before dusk. And you'd hear things... little things. What's being said in the kitchens. Who's come from Thebes? What's troubling the court?"

She finally looked up, eyes sharp with interest. "It's an excellent place to plant more than onions."

Horem chuckled. "So you don't mind?"

"I think," she said softly, "that it may be the beginning of something."

He studied her. "What do you mean?"

Dinah leaned forward, her voice just above a whisper. "A way in. A presence. One day, the women of our house may know those halls better than some of the priests. One day, one of our daughters may be at the ear of someone who matters."

Her mind wandered briefly—to the future—a future where kindness and quiet strength could move as surely as any scepter. A future shaped by bread and balm and whispered wisdom in royal corridors.

She reached out and covered Horem's hand with hers.

"I'll take the job."

He nodded slowly. They smiled at each other and continued their activities in silence. That night in their small garden, under the branches of jasmine, something new began to grow.

The Children of Dinah network would soon establish it's roots.

Chapter Sixteen

The House of On

Cold Silence

The home of Potiphera, former High Priest of On, was a place of silence and stone—its halls cool, its windows shaded by hanging gardens. The walls bore symbols of Ra and Amun, carved in alabaster and trimmed with gold.

Joseph entered with Asenath at his side, dressed not as the Vizier but as a father.

They were received in the private chamber, where Asenath's eldest brother, Nekhi, already waited with two of their uncles—men robed in fine linen and marked by suspicion. Potiphera himself sat upon a cushioned chair, aged but watchful.

Asenath knelt before her father, but there was tension in the room. The greetings were polite, but hollow.

Joseph spoke first. "We've come to share good news. Ephraim and Manasseh are to marry."

A silence fell... unseen but heavy.

Asenath lifted her eyes. "They've chosen daughters of Benjamin. Hebrew girls, born of my husband's people. Their names are Rachel and Tirzah."

Her brother stood abruptly. "You brought us here for this!"

Potiphera's brow furrowed. "You would bind our priestly line to shepherds?"

"They are not mere shepherds," Joseph said, evenly. "They are daughters of Israel. And women of wisdom."

Nekhi scoffed. "They are not daughters of Egypt."

"We sheltered those boys under our roof," another uncle added, voice rising. "And this is how you repay our care?"

"I did not ask you to raise them," Asenath said sharply. "You tolerated them, barely."

Her father lifted his hand. "Enough."

The room stilled. Potiphera turned to his daughter. "Asenath," he said quietly, "you are still of On, even if your heart is bound elsewhere. But the boys you raised—these half Hebrews are also half Egptian. You would let them shame your lineage? You would allow great destinies in Egypt to die?"

Asenath rose to her feet. "No," she said. "Both of them will fulfill their destinies."

Joseph rose and placed a gentle hand on her back.

Potiphera looked to him and then back at his daughter. "Then do what you must. But you will do it without us."

Joseph moved towards the door without a word, nodding respectfully—too respectfully, it seemed. His silence was sharper than rebuke. He bowed once to Potiphera, then turned and walked out with the grace of a man who had nothing to prove. The doors closed softly behind him.

Asenath remained.

She turned slowly to face them—not just her father, uncles, and brother, but also the weight of her past, her family name, her family's gods.

"You ask me why," she said, her voice tight. "Why would I allow my sons to marry Hebrew daughters? Why I honor the name of Israel?"

She stepped forward.

"Because while Egypt gave me birth, it was not Egypt who saved me. You forget how many times the priests of this house tried to kill Joseph! How many spells were cast in the night! How many warnings I received from servants too afraid to speak aloud."

Her gaze cut to Nekhi. "You looked me in the eye, knowing assassins were sent after my sons. You said nothing!" Her voice grew colder. "You remember the last time Joseph left Egypt? The way we packed by night? How I hid the boys with your servants? We were hunted, and you stood silent."

The men stared at her, blank expressions.

"And still," she continued, voice rising, "Joseph preserved your grain. His hands kept your temples open and your families fed. His wisdom saved your throne."

She turned to her father. "Father, the people you call shepherds—I trust them with my life. I've watched them stand by us when your own priests would not. I've seen their faith move mountains. Their God, Elohim, has answered prayers that your gods have ignored."

Potiphera's body language did not change. He was empty and motionless like the statues in his hallways, but his hands slowly tightened around the arms of his chair.

"I will not beg you to come," Asenath said. I will not let Egypt's silence mar our joy. Let it be known: the daughters of Benjamin will be my daughters, and Elohim will be my God."

She turned and strode from the chamber without another word.

Potiphera did not rise. He did not bless her. And behind him, the men stood like stone walls—silent, proud, unmoved.

Outside, the sun met her face like a blessing. Joseph waited in the carriage, his eyes searching hers.

But before she descended the final steps, something made her pause.

She turned slowly, her silks catching in the stone-carved wind, glancing up toward the shaded balcony above the courtyard. There stood her mother, partially shaded behind a lattice curtain. Their eyes met.

She did not speak. She did not wave. Her face was solemn, her chin lifted, not in defiance, but in silent resolve. A mother choosing legacy over the child who bore it forward differently.

Asenath gave a slight nod, grief and clarity mingling behind her eyes. She turned again and crossed the courtyard quickly. Joseph reached for her hand as she climbed into the carriage.

"Well?" he asked gently.

She settled beside him. "We'll not speak of it again."

And as the wheels turned, the House of On shrank behind them—quiet, gilded, and cold.

The past had closed its door. But ahead, the future waited, wide as covenant.

Chapter Seventeen

THE THRONE CHANGES HANDS

Pharaoh Dies

The black sails of mourning fluttered above the palace of Memphis as the body of Pharaoh was carried through the gates. Lamentation filled the streets, drums echoing like the heartbeat of a dying god.

Joseph stood among the dignitaries in the Hall of the Two Thrones, dressed in mourning linen, his Vizier's seal still pinned to his chest—a symbol of the trust now passing away with a Pharaoh, and a door quietly closing in his heart.

The Pharaoh who had trusted him—who had lifted him from the pit and placed him over all Egypt—was gone.

When the procession ended and the priests retreated into the embalming hall, a servant approached Joseph with a low bow.

"Pharaoh requests your presence, my lord."

Pharaoh's Final Gift

The chamber was smaller than his father's grand hall, yet no less dignified. The afternoon light streamed through open lattice windows, casting golden bars across polished stone. The young Pharaoh stood quietly, hands clasped behind his back, his crown resting beside him on a carved obsidian pedestal.

Joseph entered in silence. Despite his age, he still carried himself with the commanding respect of a Vizier of Egypt. But something in his step was slower now — more measured, more final.

Pharaoh turned at once. "Vizier."

Joseph bowed deeply. "Pharaoh."

They stood a moment, observing one another not as ruler and subject, but as men who had weathered storms together — one beginning his reign, the other nearing his end.

"You served my father with distinction," Pharaoh said. "You held this kingdom upright during its darkest years. You could have claimed glory. You never did."

Joseph said nothing, only nodded with respect.

Pharaoh exhaled and spoke softly, "But Egypt is changing, Joseph. We both know it. And I would not see you caught beneath the tide."

Joseph met his gaze with quiet resolve. "Then let me move with it."

Pharaoh stepped closer. "Twelve moons from today. You may step back in peace. The seal will pass when you say the time is right."

He paused, then added meaningfully, "And before you go, I offer this—any favor. Anything that your heart would see done before your name is etched into memory. I've heard the people speak," Pharaoh said. "To them, you are an Egyptian. Not merely by title but by spirit."

Joseph gave a faint smile. "I am Israel's son, but Egypt's servant."

"What shall Egypt give its most faithful Vizier?"

Joseph hesitated only a moment.

"Grant me this," he said. "Let the tribes of Israel be placed with purpose. Let my brothers take root in Egypt's commerce and labor. Let them become builders, traders, scribes, shepherds of prosperity—not just sheep. Their survival will be Egypt's strength."

Pharaoh smiled. "You ask for no riches? No statues in your image? Only a vision?"

"I ask for the future," Joseph replied. "My sons will walk these streets. That will be legacy enough."

Pharaoh's smile faded into a more solemn expression. "And I know what you gave to protect it. I know of the attempted attack on the road from Hebron. I know of Lord Ayar, who immediately vanished after the failed attempt and the whispers from the temple corridors. You did not expose it. You did not shame the crown."

"I protected the peace," Joseph said.

Pharaoh stepped forward and placed his hand over Joseph's heart.

"Then let it be known that your final year will be a year of honor. When the seal is passed, Egypt will not forget you. Nor will I."

But not all in Egypt were at peace with Joseph's legacy.

The Throne Holds Its Line

Later that evening, Pharaoh sat beneath the canopy of golden reeds in the Hall of Lotus Columns. Torches burned steadily. The scent of myrrh and frankincense drifted as the priesthood arrived—robes swaying, eyes watchful.

Pahor, youngest brother of the fallen Nefer-Ra, stepped forward first. His posture was composed, but the heat behind his eyes could not be hidden.

"My king," he intoned, bowing low. "We offer counsel during this time of transition."

Pharaoh, still in his ceremonial linen from the funeral, motioned for them to rise but did not smile.

"You have counsel?"

Pahor clasped his hands. "Vizier Joseph has announced his intention to retire. It is... timely. But there are matters to consider—his family's reach, their place in the courts, in the markets, in the libraries of Egypt—"

Pharaoh swiftly lifted his hand.

"You speak of a man who has served three full decades without scandal, corruption, or rebellion," he said firmly. "The people call him an Egyptian. They followed his decrees as if they were directly from Pharaoh."

Another priest tried to speak, but Pharaoh's gaze cut across the chamber.

"You dwell in shadows," he said, voice rising. "But I see light. The storehouses are full. Our alliances are strong. There is peace in the land—peace built by the man you would quietly undo."

Pahor opened his mouth to speak, but Pharaoh didn't let him.

"Enough." His word cracked through the hall like a whip. "You forget your place. Joseph has earned the right to retire in dignity. He has given me no reason to question his loyalty—or the legacy he leaves."

A heavy pause followed.

"Or shall I begin questioning yours?"

The priests lowered their heads. They stepped back; some trembled.

Pahor's voice returned, cautious now. "Of course, Pharaoh. Our concern lies only in what may come after."

Pharaoh gave no nod, no acknowledgment—just a cold, measured command.

"Then concern yourselves with silence."

The Priests Deliberate

Shortly after midnight, deep in the shadowed corridors of the temple's private wing, Pahor entered a quiet chamber lined with carved pillars and serpent motifs.

Candles lined the walls. The other priests were already seated, waiting.

He closed the door behind him.

"Pharaoh protects him," one muttered. "We pushed too early."

Pahor poured wine into a clay goblet. "Let him protect the man. For now."

Another priest leaned forward. "And the sons?"

Pahor's voice was colder now. "We begin with them. One by one. Let Egypt forget Joseph by forgetting those who follow him."

A final whisper passed among them, more felt than heard:

"Time will do what blades could not."

Chapter Eighteen

THE TRANSITIONAL YEAR

Foundations in the Marketplace

The sun was low over Goshen when Joseph gathered his brothers beneath a reed pavilion, out of sight of Egyptian officials and palace scribes. The call to meet had been discreet. Only the family knew why.

Scrolls lay open on the table: market maps, resource charts, transport ledgers. Ephraim and Manasseh stood beside their father, ready to record every decision.

Joseph spoke without fanfare, but with gravity.

"Egypt is shifting," he began. "The throne will hold—for now. But winds of change don't announce themselves with trumpets. They come quietly. So must we."

The brothers leaned in.

"My retirement is not yet known outside the palace," Joseph continued. "And it must remain that way. We have one year—one year to prepare our children for a future Egypt may not give freely."

He motioned to the scrolls. "Each of you will take a place in the commerce of the land. Not as shepherds. As men of skill. Influence. Provision."

One by one, he gave out appointments:

Reuben was placed in oversight of livestock trading posts stretching east of Goshen.

Simeon would supervise construction contracts and labor assignments in the district near Memphis.

Levi, with his natural precision, would oversee the scribal school project launching in the hill districts.

Judah was positioned over grain distribution and reserve storage across the western Delta.

Issachar was tasked with developing artisan training workshops near the temple zone.

Zebulun was assigned port authority in Nile barge transportation.

Dan was placed near security and regional guard provisioning.

Naphtali would serve in the courier and message networks between the palace and provinces.

Gad managed the distribution of weapons and oversaw the issuance of blacksmith trading permits.

Asher was positioned over the importation of spices and oils, catering to temple and noble estates.

Benjamin continued his service in administrative oversight at Goshen's treasury quarter.

Joseph looked around at them, his voice steady. "Your stations are not just labor. They are lifelines — for our children, for their children. We must not be easily removed when the tide changes."

The brothers nodded, each man sobered by the weight of trust—and the urgency.

That evening, back at the estate, Joseph and Asenath walked the fig-lined garden in silence until lanterns were lit. They paused at the fountain where Ephraim and Manasseh now sat with Rachel and Tirzah, Benjamin's daughters.

Asenath spoke first.

"They look ready. Steady. Like they were born for this."

Joseph nodded slowly. "The harvest ends in three moons. Let the wedding come just before the season closes. Before anything else begins to shift."

Asenath smiled. "A double wedding. Before the first winds of winter. Let it mark the end of what was—and the beginning of what must come."

After the Celebration

The carriage wheels turned slowly along the torchlit path, the evening air thick with the sweet scent of lilies and crushed fig leaves. Inside, Joseph leaned back against the cushions, a rare smile lingering on his face. Asenath sat beside him, her fingers loosely twined in his.

The music of the wedding still echoed faintly in their ears—the laughter, the blessings, the sound of two sons pledging themselves to two daughters, both families rejoicing.

"They were radiant," Asenath said, gazing out the small window. "All four of them."

Joseph nodded. "I don't remember my heart being this full."

She looked at him gently. "Even after all these years?"

He chuckled softly. "Especially after all these years."

They rode in silence for a while, letting the joy settle between them like warm wine.

When they arrived at the palace courtyard, the estate was already cloaked in quiet. No servants. No scribes. The lamps in the corridor shimmering low. The reception had gone late, and the city beyond had long since fallen asleep.

They walked the halls slowly, hand in hand, robes whispering over the polished stone. Each step echoed louder in the silence.

"I had forgotten what quiet sounded like," Joseph murmured.

"No, you just hadn't listened in a long time," Asenath replied, with a soft smile.

They reached their chambers, the tall doors left slightly ajar. A breeze passed through the open windows, lifting the edge of the curtains.

Joseph held the door for her, then followed her in.

As soon as it closed behind them, Asenath kicked off her sandals and spun in a slow circle, her bracelets clinking. "I don't think I stopped smiling the entire wedding," she laughed.

Joseph loosened his sash and leaned against the wall with a grin. "You danced with Manasseh. Twice."

"And you with Rachel!" she teased, poking him in the ribs. "You nearly stepped on her veil."

"She's fast on her feet. Like her mother's family," Joseph said, eyes glinting.

They both laughed—full and free—the way they hadn't in years. No titles. No court. No scribes. Just joy and the feeling of a well-written chapter.

Joseph leaned in and kissed her forehead. "If this is what retirement feels like, I should have done it sooner."

"Don't you dare," she warned playfully, then pulled him by the hand toward their bed.

They fell onto the cushions like newlyweds, limbs tangled, hearts light. For once, the weight of Egypt did not follow them into the room.

Tonight, they were only husband and wife.

Tonight, they were free.

Growth

Smoke from the early fires curled above the rooftops of Goshen, carrying the scent of baking bread, crushed grain, and morning dew on linen. Children's voices echoed from the stone-walled school near the well—their chants of letters and numbers rising like birdsong.

This was no longer a land of wandering tents. It was becoming a settlement with rhythm, responsibility, and roots.

Joseph walked to the edge of the central road, arms folded behind his back as he watched a pair of wagons roll by. This one loaded with clay jars of oil from Asher's trade depot, the other with bolts of dyed linen bound for the palace quarter.

He said nothing but noted everything.

His brothers had taken to their posts with greater energy than he expected. Gad now had a small forge operating outside the city gate, his sons assisting blacksmiths in sharpening tools and plow blades. Naphtali's network of messengers kept tabs on grain shipments, guard patrols, and festival schedules across three districts.

On the far side of Goshen, Reuben's household had turned its pasture into a model for livestock rotation—his grandsons managing the pens while the older sons supervised young boys from other tribes.

The school had opened quietly in the spring. It was modest holding three rooms, one scroll cabinet, and a teaching platform but it was always filled. Levi supervised the instructors with sharp discipline, while Issachar sent his daughters daily to assist the little ones in learning their letters.

In the evenings, the courtyard of Joseph's estate glowed with lamplight as Asenath and Dinah worked steadily at the long table, sorting family records, songs, laws, and stories. What began as preservation had become a quiet obsession. One night, Dinah leaned over a scroll and whispered, "This isn't just for us. This is for the ones who won't remember how it felt to be free."

Asenath replied without lifting her pen, "Then we write it, so they do."

Joseph often paused to watch them from the colonnade, two women shaping legacy by hand.

In the palace, Joseph began quietly surveying his replacement-not from among the highborn, but from the ranks of younger scribes, men who had grown under his leadership. He observed how they listened, how they made decisions under pressure, and which ones ruled with justice rather than pride.

Pharaoh gave him full liberty. "The next Vizier will follow your ways," he'd said. "But he will never be your equal."

Joseph had only smiled. "Nor should he try. Egypt will not need another me. It will need someone who understands the days to come."

And so the year moved on, not in grand declarations, but in the steady rhythm of legacy being passed like a torch—quiet, hot, and enduring.

Chapter Nineteen

SEASONS OF JOY AND SILENCE

Family Time

Joseph retired without ceremony. No seal returned in a public hall, no fanfare from the palace gates. He stopped wearing the Vizier's ring, and Pharaoh, out of respect for Joseph's wishes, said nothing.

The year had shifted, and so had Joseph. His walks grew shorter, his robes simpler. He no longer carried scrolls but grandchildren.

Manasseh's wife, Rachel, bore twins in the spring—two sons with eyes like their grandfather's and quiet strength in their tiny fists. Joseph wept when he held them, whispering blessings from the old country, words his father once spoke over him.

Ephraim and Tirzah named their first daughter Keziyah, after a flowering spice. She walked before she spoke and laughed like Asenath did when she was young.

The days were full — markets thriving, schools expanding, scrolls multiplying. The family had taken root not just in Egypt, but in purpose. Hebrew boys now worked beside Egyptian craftsmen. Hebrew girls studied law beside the Nile.

And yet, as the tribes grew, the brothers' numbers dwindled.

Levi was the first to go. One morning, he didn't get out of bed. His hands still held a teaching stick, scrolls stacked at the foot of his mat.

Naphtali followed in the winter, the cold settling too deep in his bones.

Dan died just after the planting season, his sons taking over the security and guard provisioning without pause.

There was no wailing in the streets. No sackcloth. Just quiet mourning. And the work that went on—because that's what they would have wanted. Joseph stood beneath a fig tree one afternoon, Keziyah on his shoulders, watching Ephraim repair a clay channel with Benjamin's eldest son.

"Everything is changing," Asenath said gently, walking up beside him.

Joseph nodded. "And yet... we're still here."

The Last Garden Gathering

Two and a half decades had passed since Joseph stepped away from the halls of power.

The years had been generous. His sons had risen in stature. His grandchildren had filled the homes and courts of Goshen. His family was no longer just a presence in Egypt—they were a foundation.

One of his great nephews was already a father. The child, born just weeks after Reuben's passing, had been named Reuben—a quiet tribute to the firstborn who had once tried to save his younger brother so long ago. The name carried sorrow and redemption in equal measure.

Early one morning, word had passed like wind among the tribes: Joseph is calling for us.

There was no ceremony. No public summons. Just a message passed from house to house: Come. It is time.

By mid-afternoon, they gathered in the inner garden of Joseph's estate, under the olive trees he had planted during his first years in Egypt. Their trunks had thickened, twisted, and aged like the family itself—deep-rooted, fruitful, and marked by the passage of time.

Joseph sat bundled in a heavy cloak, his shoulders thin beneath the fabric. The Vizier's seal had long been set aside, replaced now by a wooden walking staff resting against his chair. His hair was silver, his hands gnarled by age, but his eyes—those same eyes that once interpreted dreams and calmed kings—were still clear and bright.

At his side, Asenath held his hand, her other hand resting gently on his knee. Her face was lined with years, but her presence remained regal, dignified. She wept without sobbing, her heart too full for words.

Joseph turned his head slowly, scanning the circle around him—an entire generation and more, gathered in silence.

He first saw Benjamin, still strong though deeply aged, the last of their mother Rachel's children. His eyes glistened. Their bond had never weakened.

Judah stood next to him, upright and proud, the quiet authority of the family now resting on his shoulders. Joseph nodded to him, and Judah bowed his head in return.

He found Ephraim and Manasseh standing near one another, their wives at their sides, and their children gathered close. Manasseh's twin boys flanked him like young soldiers; Ephraim's daughter Keziyah clung to his tunic. Joseph's chest rose gently with pride.

He looked for each of his brothers—Simeon, Issachar, Zebulun, Asher, and Gad—now older, weathered by both age and the demands of leadership. They had buried Levi, Naphtali, Dan, and Reuben. But those still living had honored their callings.

Each man nodded when Joseph's eyes met theirs. And behind them stood their children and their grandchildren, a river of faces born of sorrow, survival, and hope.

His gaze paused on Kiya and Nari, Dinah's stepdaughters.

Horam had passed a few years ago, though not before entrusting the tailor shop to Nira and her husband—ensuring the craft would remain in faithful hands.

Dinah had followed only last year, her kindness and quiet wisdom now living on in the ones she had called her own.

The girls had married kind-hearted Egyptians—men who honored Elohim in word and in deed. Their children sat nearby, still and watchful, their dark curls catching the evening light.

Joseph smiled softly, his heart warmed by their presence, and by the legacy Dinah had left behind.

He drew a slow, measured breath.

"I have lived to see the promises of Elohim stretch beyond my father's tent," he said, his voice low but even. "You are no longer only sons of Israel. You are tribes. A people."

The silence deepened.

"But I am about to die," he said. "And though Egypt has been a land of peace, this is not our home."

He reached for Asenath's hand, his fingers trembling slightly. She squeezed gently.

"God will surely come to you," Joseph said. "He will not leave you here forever. When He comes—when He delivers you—do not leave me behind."

He looked around again. "Swear to me... You will carry my bones with you."

Benjamin stepped forward first. Then Judah. Then one by one, each of the living brothers and eldest sons came and placed their hand over his.

"We swear it," they said, in voices steady and solemn.

Tears slipped down Asenath's cheeks.

Joseph leaned back against the chair, looking up at the olive branches swaying softly above him. His breath slowed. His smile lingered.

"You gave me Egypt," he whispered to her.

She leaned close. "And you gave me eternity."

And the garden, full of generations and memory, held its breath in reverence.

The Mourning of Two

There was no secrecy in his death.

When the word reached Pharaoh, the court was called to attention. Banners were lowered across Memphis and Thebes, and for the first time in memory, the mourning rites of a Vizier were extended to a foreign-born son.

Joseph was embalmed with the care reserved only for nobility and kings. Linen was wound with myrrh and aloes, each layer a gesture of honor and remembrance.

His body was not hidden deep within a palace tomb or sealed inside a royal catacomb.

Instead, Joseph's coffin was placed at the edge of Goshen, facing the main road that led to the capital. A carved pavilion sheltered the ornate box, its wooden panels engraved with scenes from both Hebrew and Egyptian life—his coat of many colors, the sheaves of wheat, the seal of Pharaoh, and the words of Jacob's blessing.

Travelers stopped. Farmers bowed. Merchants crossed themselves. Even the priests, though quietly bitter, did not protest.

All who passed by would know: A great man rested here.

But only a week into the time of mourning, as if her heart could not go on beating without his beside it, Asenath passed in her sleep. No pain. No sound. Only stillness.

The household was hushed. Double mourning draped the walls.

The women wore dark veils. The children did not laugh for many days. Even the olive trees seemed to sway slower under the weight of their absence.

Ephraim and Manasseh buried her near the pavilion—not in a temple graveyard, but beside the man she chose, and the God she came to love.

Chapter Twenty

EPILOGUE – THE MOSES CHRONICLES BEGIN

Memories and Legacies

Years passed. Then decades. Then generations.

The children of Israel prospered and multiplied. Their roots grew deep in the soil of Goshen, and their presence spread like vines along the edges of Egypt's cities. Their flocks increased, their harvests grew heavy, and their sons filled courts, fields, and scroll halls.

Egypt, meanwhile, faced its own turning. Pharaohs died. Dynasties rose and fell. Some ruled with wisdom, others with blood. And through it all, the name of Joseph remained—spoken in quiet reverence among the Hebrews and remembered in silence by Egypt's aging walls.

The pavilion that marked his resting place remained untouched, a stone sentinel on the road between Goshen and the palace. Children were brought there to hear the stories. Elders wept there when sons were born or buried.

Asenath's grave remained beside his. The woman who had bridged two nations was never forgotten.

And then, a whisper began—soft, uncertain, but real.

A Hebrew. In the palace. Again.

Another story is about to begin.

1 These are the names of the sons of Israel who came to Egypt with Jacob, each with his household: 2 Reuben,

Simeon, Levi, and Judah, 3 Issachar, Zebulun, and Benjamin, 4 Dan and Naphtali, Gad and Asher. 5 All the descendants of Jacob were seventy persons; Joseph was already in Egypt. 6 Then Joseph died, and all his brothers and all that generation. 7 **But the people of Israel were fruitful and increased greatly; they multiplied and grew exceedingly strong, so that the land was filled with them.**▫

8 **Now there arose a new king over Egypt, who did not know Joseph.**— Exodus 1:1–8

Want more of the story?
Come behind the curtain.
Get early access to upcoming chapters, behind-the-scenes updates, and the sacred echoes between the verses.
Free bonus content + book news at **MosesChronicles.com**
You've walked beside Joseph, Dinah, and Asenath.
But their legacy is only the beginning.
The prelude has ended.
The deliverer has not yet been born.
Continue the journey.
One book down—seven still to come.

Stay Connected

To explore behind-the-scenes reflections, upcoming bookannouncements,
or teaching series inspired by *The Moses Chronicles*,follow:
Email: Regina@MosesChronicles.com
Website: www.MosesChronicles.com
Instagram / **Facebook**: @TheMosesChronicles
YouTube: Search "RR Wekesa" or "The Moses Chronicles"

JOIN THE SCRIBE CIRCLE NEWSLETTER

About the Author

Regina V. Roundtree, writing as RR Wekesa, is drawn to the quiet spaces in Scripture—where hearts break, heal, and walk with God. Her first novel, The Moses Chronicles: Prelude, *launched an eight-book biblical fiction series that reimagines deliverance through the voices of those who lived it. Her second volume,* Hands That Rock theCradle, *continues that journey with reverence, imagination, and prophetic depth.*

She writes not from titles, but from reverence. Not to instruct, but to inspire. Her work is shaped by a journey of healing, Torah rediscovery, and global faith—having lived and studied acrosst he U.S., Zambia, Kenya, South Africa, and Southeast Asia.

Through The Moses Chronicles, *she brings vibrance to the relationships that shaped both history and hope—inviting readers to listen for the voices between the verses.*